Exe Factor

Suzy Bussell

Chapter One

Charlotte Lockwood entered The Ivy restaurant in the centre of Exeter nearly half an hour late. She was flustered and tetchy, because she hated being late as much as she hated her cheating ex-husband. It was especially galling today of all days because she was meeting Katrina, an old friend from her university days.

She stood just inside the doorway and glanced around, then spied Katrina at a table by the window and headed over.

The Ivy had only recently opened in what had been a bank, then a clothing store. Now the Victorian white stone building was a posh restaurant.

The magnificent high ceiling made it feel special. Tall indoor plants contrasted with the white tablecloths. The chairs had an ivy pattern, and a tastefully decorated bar had been made out of what had been bank-teller desks. At the far end, on a low stage, a man played soft classical music on a grand piano.

When Charlotte approached, Katrina was staring wistfully at her half-full coffee cup.

"Hello, darling, so sorry I'm late. That horrible accident meant we had to go the long way, but I'm here now." She had already messaged Katrina to tell her that she was stuck in traffic, but she still thought an explanation was required.

Katrina stood up and they kissed each other on the cheek, then sat down. Katrina was the same age as Charlotte: in her mid-forties. Charlotte had always envied Katrina's naturally curly brown hair, which had a few grey strands at the front now.

"I love your dress," Charlotte said, admiring the pink-and-red-floral pattern. She herself wore smart navy trousers and a loose white top.

"Thank you, and it's all right, my love. You can't help these things, can you? What are you having, tea?" Katrina handed Charlotte the menu and she browsed it.

"Eggs Benedict with a pot of breakfast tea." Charlotte had skipped breakfast on purpose to eat it here.

Katrina waved at a waitress, who came over and took Charlotte's order. When she was gone, Charlotte scanned Katrina's face. It had been nearly a year since they'd seen each other. Every time they'd tried to meet, one of them had to cancel. She tried to remember when meeting friends had been less complicated. It seemed that the older you got, the harder it was to meet up with people.

Since they'd last met, Charlotte had started working as a private detective with ex-policeman Angus Darrow. Their relationship was strictly professional, which was annoying since Charlotte already had deeper feelings for Angus, however much she tried to deny them.

Katrina put her hands over her face for a moment, then removed them and stared at Charlotte. "You need to help me. I've been the biggest idiot ever. I've done something really stupid."

Charlotte shifted in her seat. "What is it?" Her mind quickly ran through a few scenarios. Murder? Theft? Judging by the dark patches under Katrina's eyes and the worried look on her face, this was serious.

"I've been catfished."

"Catfished? What happened?" Charlotte knew all about catfishing from her time as a cybersecurity expert. Catfishers set up a fake account and pretended to be romantically interested in their target, but it was always a ruse to get money from them. She looked into Katrina's eyes and saw the pain.

Katrina stared down at her coffee cup. "It started a few months ago; he replied to my post in a Facebook group about getting over the death of a pet. Then he messaged me privately. We chatted and talked for days."

Typical catfisher tactic, thought Charlotte. Lull the target into a false sense of security by talking to them intensely for days, even weeks. "How long before he started with the compliments?" she asked.

"I can't remember. Not long." Katrina drained her coffee cup. "I was flattered. It's been such a long time since any man showed me that amount of attention. Any attention, to be honest. When I broke up with Neil, I didn't think any man would be interested in me again. It was such a toxic relationship."

The waitress interrupted them with Charlotte's tea things. Katrina watched Charlotte pour herself a cup.

"He was so nice, and I got addicted to messaging him. We talked about everything. He talked about his family and his plans for the future."

"Where did he say he lived?"

"Newcastle. He said he was just out of a relationship."

3

Charlotte shook her head gently. "They always say they're single. Did you send him money?"

After a pause, Katrina nodded.

"How much?" Charlotte wasn't sure she wanted to know.

"Twenty thousand pounds ... all my savings."

Charlotte sat back in her chair, shut her eyes and sighed. "Oh, Katrina, what were you thinking?"

Katrina burst into tears, and several of the other diners glanced over as she sobbed.

Charlotte stood up and moved her chair next to Katrina's, then put her arm around her. "I'm sorry."

It took Katrina a few minutes to calm down, and Charlotte continued to hug her. "I'm sorry," Katrina said, wiping her eyes. It was a good thing she wasn't wearing much makeup; mascara would have been streaming down her cheeks. Charlotte passed Katrina a napkin and she dabbed her eyes. "It's just so humiliating. I'm so ashamed."

"Hey, there's no need to be ashamed. I didn't mean to be so harsh; it's just that you've always been so astute and wise. Anyway, it's not your fault. You're the victim here, and I don't like victim-blaming. It was wrong of me."

Katrina managed a half-smile.

The waitress came with Charlotte's food, so she moved back to her place. The eggs Benedict looked and smelt delicious, and she eagerly started to eat as Katrina continued on. Katrina sighed. "I can't believe I was so stupid. Looking back now, it's obvious. I've been so lonely, more than I realised and I was flattered. I should have known it was too good to be true. He said he was thirty-eight, and from the pictures, that looked right, but it was all made up, wasn't it?"

Charlotte nodded. "Catfishers never use a real profile. He could be anyone: a man or a woman."

"He said he ran a string of gyms. I Googled, and he had a website and everything. But that was fake too. I should have known; he was gorgeous and he kept posting pictures of himself."

"What did he say to get you to send him money?"

"He said he was investing in a housing development. He didn't mention it much to start with, but then he said he'd made a hundred thousand pounds before and he had the opportunity again. I asked him about it, and he mentioned an app you can invest in."

"You downloaded the app?"

Katrina nodded. "It all looked legit, so I set up an account and sent my money."

"Let me guess: the moment you sent the money he disappeared, and you haven't heard from him since."

Katrina started crying again, but this time they were silent tears.

Charlotte felt anger growing inside her. She'd grown used to clearing up the mess of criminal activity when she'd worked in her cybersecurity company, but this sort of scam never failed to shock and distress her. And it was ten times worse because it was Katrina, a woman who'd do no harm to anyone. They'd met at university in Exeter. Charlotte had been studying computing, Katrina history. They'd had rooms next to each other in halls, struck up a friendship, and stayed in touch for over twenty-five years.

"Have you reported it to the police?" she asked.

"Yes. They were understanding, but they said there wasn't much they could do except log it. They're over-stretched, and the volume of cybercrimes is growing."

True, thought Charlotte. The cybersecurity industry was short-staffed. Cybersecurity could be a job for life, but most people weren't aware or willing to put in the effort. It was frustrating, especially when she knew plenty of women with side hustles like selling cosmetics or perfume, scraping by with a few quid here and there. They could retrain and earn stacks of cash.

"I'll give you the money they took," Charlotte blurted out. She didn't have to think twice about it; twenty thousand pounds was nothing to her. She was a multimillionaire, having sold her cybersecurity business a few years ago for two hundred million pounds. Admittedly, she'd only got half of that. Her husband had got the other half, which was only fair, since they'd started the company together and worked for years to make it a success. What she had resented was him running off with her best friend, Michelle, the moment the sale went through.

Katrina stared at her. "I didn't ask you here to beg for money, Charlotte. I want you to find the bastard and stop him doing this to someone else."

Charlotte was, momentarily, speechless. She looked down at her food, assembled a forkful and took a bite. It tasted divine.

They sat in silence for a few moments as Charlotte ate. Eventually, she put her knife and fork down. "I'll do the best I can, but I should warn you that the people behind these scams are usually abroad: in Russia or somewhere similar. Even if I do find them, there's probably nothing we can do."

Katrina looked wistfully out of the window at the street outside. Charlotte's gaze followed hers to a street seller with a small barrow, loaded with mobile-phone accessories.

"I shouldn't have let my feelings overrule my head," said Katrina. "You're still working as a private investigator, aren't you?"

"I am." Charlotte couldn't help smiling.

"Just you?"

"No, I'm under the guidance of an ex-police officer, Angus Darrow. He's fabulous, but don't tell him I said that." Charlotte giggled.

"How did you get into it?"

"He needed a computer expert. I was free." She gave a small shrug. "He doesn't pay me, but that's fine. It stops me stewing over Idris and Michelle."

"I still can't believe he left you for your best friend. I never liked Idris. He always put you down."

Charlotte didn't say anything. Plenty of her friends and family had said similar things when her marriage had gone down the pan. If so many people thought Idris was no good for her, no one had ever said it when they were together.

"I wanted your help because I don't want other people falling victim to him."

Charlotte took another sip of tea. "You won't be their first victim or their last, probably, but I'll do my best. I'll need access to all communications between you and him."

Katrina winced. "All of it?"

"All of it."

"But it's so embarrassing; you'll think I'm a total fool. Is there no way you can find out without reading it all?"

"Look, I won't judge you, but everything he sent may hold a clue to his real identity. A digital trace."

Katrina groaned. "You promise not to let anyone else see it – and I mean no one?"

Charlotte's thoughts immediately went to her partner and fellow private investigator, Angus. He was a technophobe; she did all the computer work. She couldn't think of a reason why he would need to read any of it. Usually she just reported the important information to him without the technobabble. Occasionally she tried to teach him some basics, but his eyes always glazed over. She hadn't given up hope that he might be interested one day. "I promise," she said.

Katrina sighed deeply. "Oh, darling, thank you so much. I don't know what I would do without you."

Charlotte gave a dismissive wave. "Give me your phone and I'll download the messages."

It took Charlotte half an hour to get everything. The messages had started on Facebook Messenger, then moved to WhatsApp. The catfisher had used the name Marcus Fielder. Judging by the photos, he'd either stolen someone's identity or had a model pose for him. Probably a stolen ID, thought Charlotte. With so many people trying to get their dose of serotonin from likes or shares on social media, there were always plenty of real-life people to steal photos from. That was what she would do if she was criminally inclined. It was also the reason why she didn't post pictures of herself on social media.

"Are you sure there was no other way you talked to him? Text, email?"

"No, that's everything." Katrina stood up.

"I'll keep you posted." Charlotte stood up, too, and kissed her on the cheek. Then she sat back down to think over Katrina's problem. She could do several things to try and find the catfisher. If those failed, she knew a couple of people who worked in social media and owed her a favour or two. That could wait a few hours, though. She checked her watch. If she hurried, she could meet up with Angus.

Chapter Two

Grigore arrived a few minutes later in Charlotte's Bentley. He pulled up outside the restaurant, got out of the driver's seat and opened the door for her. He was a burly man in his late twenties. Not only was he her driver, but also a kind of bodyguard, handyman and general muscle. Charlotte paid him very well, but she thought the world of Grigore: he'd proved his honesty so many times in the past few years. She didn't know what she would do if he decided to leave.

The Bentley caused a small stir on the high street as people stared, wondering who the lady with the smart car and driver was.

"You go home?" Grigore asked in his thick Romanian accent, once they were both in the car.

"No, I want to see Angus."

He nodded, and the car pulled smoothly away.

During the short journey, Charlotte skimmed the messages between Katrina and the catfisher. They were just as Katrina had described: friendly at first, then more and more chatty, incorporating flattery which turned into amorous and overstated adulation. It was sickening to see how the catfisher had manipulated her friend at a time when she was vulnerable and lonely. Well, she would leave no stone unturned to find them.

Angus heard the doorbell ring and knew who it was.

"Hello, I called but it went to voicemail," said Charlotte as soon as he opened the door, standing with one hand on her hip."You look dashing as usual," she added looking him up and down. She was carrying two takeaway coffee cups in a holder. Angus was average height, just under six foot with dark-brown hair which had some grey scattered in it. He was slim because he liked to keep himself fit by running. As usual, he was dressed in suit trousers and a crisp white shirt, but wore no tie. He hadn't planned on going out, but he always hated looking scruffy, even at home.

He pushed his glasses up his nose. "I was out running earlier, but I thought you'd drop by. Come in."

He'd seen her call, and hadn't called her back. If he'd learnt one thing over the last few months, it was that if Charlotte needed to speak to him, she wouldn't let a silly thing like him not answering the phone get in the way. He liked it.

She stepped inside and went through to the kitchen. When Angus closed the door, he saw Grigore in the Bentley. Their eyes met and they nodded at each other.

"Grigore not coming in?" Angus said as he entered the kitchen. Grigore had never come into Angus's house. He always stayed with the Bentley, parked outside or disappeared off to who-knows-where.

"No, he'll be back later. He has to fill the car up with fuel."

"That sounds expensive."

Charlotte sat down at the breakfast bar and handed him a coffee cup. "Yes. So you were out running again?"

"Yep. Still training for the Grizzly."

Charlotte grimaced. "Grizzly is the right name for it. I can't believe you want to race twenty-three miles over roads, fields and beaches. It's like a horrible school cross-country."

Angus chuckled. "You should try it with me sometime. It clears your mind, running in the middle of nowhere."

"I can't imagine anything worse. Not with you, I mean, but the running. I'd just hold you back."

"Tell you what, if you come on a training run with me, I'll let you teach me some tech."

Charlotte's eyes narrowed suspiciously. "How much tech?"

"However long you run for, I'll spend learning about bits and bobs."

"Bits and bytes, Angus." Charlotte laughed. "It's bytes, not bobs."

"There's still plenty of time, if you change your mind." He sat down at the breakfast bar. "So, what did you want to speak to me about?"

Charlotte looked at him over her coffee cup. "I have something I need to look into." And she told him about Katrina and the catfisher.

Angus sipped his coffee as she spoke: a white Americano, easy on the milk. "Romance scams are among the most common frauds now," he said, turning the cup in his hand. "When I first started out in the police, scams like this were done in person. The scammer had to work over a long period of time to get their victim's trust. And the victims were usually very rich." He looked at Charlotte. She was very rich. He wondered how many people had tried to scam her. "These days, they'll try anyone they can."

Charlotte got off her stool and paced around the room. "Katrina isn't stupid, but she's lonely. I should have checked up on her sooner. We call each other every few weeks, but she didn't mention she was talking to someone online."

"Maybe she wanted to see where it went before telling you."

Charlotte nodded. "I'll analyse the photos and do what I can, but I'm pretty sure he'll be abroad, in a country where there's no extradition."

Angus dreaded to think what Charlotte would have to do to analyse the photos; he was a stickler for detail in everything but technology. He was starting to regret challenging her to train with him; if she did, he'd have to learn some technobabble. "Let me know if you find anything important."

She smiled and sat back down. "How's the insurance fraud investigation going?"

Angus had got the case through a friend of a friend, and it was right up his street: a supposed burglary involving the theft of pictures and jewellery from a stately home just outside Plymouth. He was busy delving into the circumstances behind the theft and the family who were claiming. There wasn't much for Charlotte to do.

"Good. It's still hush-hush; the family don't know they're being investigated. I haven't spoken to them yet, but I will eventually."

"Do you think it's dodgy?"

Angus pondered; he'd been asking himself the same question. "I'm not sure. They've taken all the right steps so far. They had photographic proof of the items, receipts dating back nearly eighty years, and recent valuations. It could be legit: they're a well-known family and their house is historic. But they've been struggling financially, so that's a red flag."

"Recent valuations?" Charlotte raised her eyebrows.

"I know. That's what the insurance company were concerned about, and why they asked me to look into it."

"Is there anything you need me to do?"

Angus shook his head. "Not at the moment, but I'll let you know if anything crops up."

Charlotte nodded. "Well, I'd better get going. I'll keep you posted."

"Likewise, and thanks for the coffee."

He saw her out, and watched the Bentley disappear. He'd been reluctant when Charlotte had first wanted to work with him; he'd been used to working alone since leaving the police. Her tech knowledge had been invaluable in so many ways, though, and since their first case, which had had a few ups and downs, they'd worked well together. Charlotte had been eager to learn everything she could about investigations, and he'd even taught her the basics of tailing someone. That had been an interesting day. They'd gone to the centre of Exeter, picked out a random person, and tailed him round the shops until he got on a bus. He'd enjoyed instructing her, and she'd been a keen student. She was good at it, too, but that didn't surprise him. Charlotte was brilliant at almost everything she put her mind to and she was growing on him. He'd found her erratic and unpredictable at first, but lately she'd mellowed, and although there was still an element of surprise with her, he liked her being around.

. . .

Charlotte went home: Fortescue House in Topsham, a small town on the River Exe between Exeter and Exmouth. The house sat in an elevated position overlooking the River Exe and was built in the Victorian period which meant the ceilings were high and the rooms large. A delicious smell of cooking hit her as soon as she opened the door, and she followed it to the kitchen.

Helena, her friend and housekeeper, was busy creating. Bowls and plates were laid out on the counters, and on the stove, various pans bubbled away. Helena was from Romania and had moved to England before Brexit. She was a little older than Charlotte, and had long brown hair she tied back in a ponytail, black leggings and a red T-shirt underneath a white chef's apron.

Charlotte kissed Helena on the cheek. "Whatever you're cooking smells amazing."

Helena shrugged. "Of course. I never cook bad, and zis vill be very special meal."

"Sounds intriguing. Who is it for?"

"It for vomen at refuge. Special midsummer meal. I tell you last veek," she said in her thick Romanian accent.

Charlotte went to the fridge, took out a bottle of tonic water and poured herself a glass. "So you did. I've got a sieve for a brain at the moment; must be the perimenopause. How are things over there?" She had set up and funded the refuge as one of her first acts of philanthropy when she became a multimillionaire. Helena worked there once a week, helping the women who came in.

"Good. Still too many vomen treated bad by man. Same story almost every time. Girl meets boy, boy controlling and nasty, girl takes long time to leave because she zink it her fault he bad. Eventually she realise it not her fault and she get avay."

Charlotte took a sip of tonic water. "It's so depressing there's no end to it."

Helena held up her wooden spoon. "But good they have place away from men to heal."

"Always the optimist, Helena."

"Alvays."

Charlotte thought about Katrina. She'd been the victim of a different kind of abuse, from a scammer. She must try and be more like Helena. "I do wonder if there's a man alive who isn't abusive. Or a cheat." She thought of her ex-husband, Idris. He'd never been abusive, but he had been a dirty rotten cheat.

Helena looked up. "Mr Angus, he nice man."

Charlotte nodded. He was more than nice.

"Grigore, he nice too," Helena added, picking up a tray of previously prepared pastries and putting it in the oven. She straightened up. "He my nephew, so I bias. Your brother, Mark, he look after you all your life, you told me."

Charlotte smiled. "You're right. A few bad men make all the others look bad."

She left Helena in the kitchen and set to work on the messages Katrina had given her, this time looking in much more detail. She started with the Facebook messages, then moved on to WhatsApp; typical of scammers to use an encrypted messaging service. It was horrible reading the messages, knowing that the person or people behind it were targeting Katrina, playing on her insecurities and her loneliness.

She searched for the profile on Facebook, and was surprised to find it still there. She tried to log in to it, but it had two-factor authentication setup. The catfisher would get a code sent to their email or phone, without the code, it wouldn't let you log in. Lots of websites used it. It was good

15

in that it stopped people being hacked, but annoying for the hacker.

Reading the messages was like reading a film script. There were lots of them, and once Katrina started to respond, they became a flood.

The photos on the Facebook profile were of a fit, attractive man in his mid-thirties, with a bodybuilder's physique. It wouldn't actually be the catfisher, but photos of some unsuspecting Instagram user who'd got addicted to posting selfies as well as pumping iron.

Reading the messages, Charlotte wondered if she would have fallen for such adoration. No. She was more cautious these days than ever. Being rich meant that she had to tread carefully with any man. Except Angus.

She'd try one more thing: analysing the photos. Some of the pictures in WhatsApp were different from the rest. They weren't selfies, for a start. She set to work downloading them onto her computer and running analysis software on them.

Chapter Three

The next day, Angus sat in the drawing room of Combpyne House. The insurance fraud investigation had progressed quickly, and now he needed to interview the claimant: Mr Perry, the owner.

The door had been answered by someone who he presumed was a member of staff: an elderly woman with a pronounced dowager's hump. He'd had to shout his name when she opened the door. She shuffled in front of him to the drawing room, and Angus spotted a hearing aid behind her ear. He wondered why she hadn't switched it on.

His guide disappeared to fetch Mr Perry, and Angus surveyed the room. It was like stepping back in time to a Victorian drawing room; some of the furniture looked as if it had been there as long as the house. The room was extremely cluttered, and he took a deep breath. He hated clutter, and antiques were no excuse. The room smelt musty, and worst of all, there were stuffed animal heads on the walls: a fox, a badger and a deer. Angus surmised it was a roe deer – a buck, because of the antlers. It was so shabby that it had no doubt met its unfortunate end decades ago.

17

The only sound was the ticking of a grandfather clock in the corner.

Mr Perry entered the room after a few minutes, and Angus stood up and shook his hand. He was in his mid-sixties, practically bald, and wore a patterned jumper and brown trousers. He waved at Angus to sit back down. "The insurance company said you had a few questions for me," he said, in a cut-glass English accent.

Angus took out his notebook and pen. "Yes, they've asked me to check some details."

By Mr Perry's frown, he didn't seem too happy about it. "I'm not sure what I wrote that they need to check. I filled out the report, which took me ages. Do they make the claim forms so long and arduous to put people off claiming?"

Yes, they do. But Angus pressed on with his first question. "I know it was on the claim form, but can you tell me, in your own words, what happened on the night of the burglary?" Angus spoke softly and pushed up his glasses.

Mr Perry shifted in his seat. "I locked up, as usual. I always lock up every night, and check every door and window. It's a routine I've followed for the last forty-five years." He watched Angus write. "Then I went to bed."

"Did you hear the burglars?"

"No. I took some diazepam, so I was out like a light."

Angus recognised the name: sleeping pills, dished out by doctors, right, left and centre. He had slept much better since leaving the police, and luckily never had to touch anything like them.

"You live alone?"

"Yes. Mrs Carter, who let you in, lives down the road."

"And how did you discover the burglary?"

Mr Perry looked towards the window. "They'd smashed

a window and climbed in. Not this window: one in the kitchen."

"Can you show me?"

Mr Perry nodded and stood up. "This way."

They went through to the kitchen, where Mrs Carter was busy washing up. Angus thought it amusing that he hadn't been offered tea or coffee, but he suspected that Mr Perry wanted him out as quickly as possible, and a hot drink would prolong things. The kitchen looked like it had been installed in the '70s. It was classic orange with garish wallpaper and a cooker that needed to be put out of its misery.

Mr Perry pointed to the window. "It was this one. They smashed it, climbed through, took what they wanted and left the same way."

Angus took out his phone and snapped a few photos. "And the police didn't come for fingerprints?"

"No," Mr Perry huffed. "Too busy dealing with the G7 summit. It was on in Torquay, and they were all protecting world leaders."

Angus remembered the summit; it had been a couple of months ago, and was big news in the area. He'd heard from his ex-colleagues that not only were Devon and Cornwall Police stretched beyond their means, but that the armed forces, MI5 and MI6 were all drafted in to deal with climate protestors, the extreme left, extreme right, flat-earthers and every crank and conspiracy theorist out there. It would have been an ideal time to fake a burglary, knowing it was unlikely the police would attend.

They were interrupted by the doorbell. Mrs Carter must have turned her hearing aid on, as she dried her hands on a tea towel and left the kitchen. She returned half a minute later. "This lady says she's here for Mr Darrow."

Angus was looking through the window to see what was

below, and whether the window was blocked by bushes or plants, then turned and saw Charlotte.

"Hello, Mr Darrow," she said, with an amused smile.

He should have known; Charlotte kept popping up in all sorts of situations. She hadn't known he was coming; he'd thought it best to go alone, as two insurance investigators seemed like overkill. He should be angry, but with one look at her beaming smile, he forgave her.

"Miss Lockwood, I thought you were looking into that other case," he said, raising his eyebrows.

"I had a breakthrough. I'll tell you about it later." She advanced and held out her hand to Mr Perry. "Charlotte Lockwood. Pleased to met you."

Mr Perry shook her hand, softening a little at the sight of an attractive blonde woman in a flowery dress. "Mr Perry," he said, in reply.

Angus turned to him. "I need to see where the stolen items were on the night they were taken, and then outside this window."

Mr Perry led them into his study. It was a large room lined with bookshelves, which were stuffed with old hardback books. Just like the rest of the house, there was a musty smell. "All the stolen items were here. They took some of my mother's jewellery – not worth much, but it had sentimental value. It was stored in this drawer." He pointed to a mahogany chest of drawers. "The items of value were my collection of vintage cameras. One was disguised as a book, another as a pocket watch."

Charlotte looked around her. It was all fascinating. "That sounds like an amazing collection. Do you think some were used by spies?"

"Absolutely. That's why I bought them." Mr Perry actually smiled. That was a first.

"I love photography," said Charlotte. "I only use a digital camera these days, but I'm old enough to remember cameras with film."

Mr Perry nodded. "I prefer old cameras; I've always been fascinated by them. The ones taken were of significant historical value."

"I'll be sure to have a good look at the photos you took. They're in the file, aren't they?" Charlotte asked Angus.

"Yes, back at the office."

"The one shaped like a pocket watch was said to have been used by one of the first MI6 operatives during World War Two," Mr Perry said. "It's not worth much money because it's in such bad condition, but I buy items for their uniqueness."

Charlotte smiled at Mr Perry, and there was a pause until Angus broke the silence. "We just need to see outside now."

"Right, yes." Mr Perry led them outside and around the house to the window where the burglars had entered.

There was a small flowerbed below the window, and the sill was easily large enough for a size ten foot. Angus took more photos as Charlotte and Mr Perry looked on. "Right, that's all. Thanks for your time, Mr Perry." Angus gave Charlotte a *We're leaving* sort of look.

Charlotte took the hint. "Right, yes. Nice to meet you, Mr Perry."

They walked to the front of the house where Angus had parked. "Grigore dropped you off?" he asked.

"Yep. You'll have to take me back to base."

Angus unlocked the car with his key fob and they both got in.

"That poor man, having his camera collection stolen," Charlotte said as soon as they had shut the doors.

"He's guilty as hell."

Charlotte stared at him. "That's so cynical!"

"No, it isn't."

"Why do you say that?"

"He claims the burglary happened during the G7 summit, when he knew that the police were unlikely to come."

"It could just be a coincidence."

"No." Angus looked through the windscreen. "I know he's lying, and the claim is false. I just need to prove it."

"Gut feeling?"

Angus nodded.

"Do you think he's hidden the cameras in the house?"

"Possibly. But if he's stored them elsewhere, there could be someone else in on it." Angus sighed. "Anyway, you said you'd had a breakthrough with your friend's catfisher?"

"Yes!" said Charlotte, elated she could finally tell him. "It took a bit of analysis, but I've located him."

Chapter Four

"Where is he? Who is he?" Angus asked.

"It is a man, and he's here in Devon."

Angus scanned her face; her eyes had brightened and she was beaming. "I thought most scammers lived abroad?"

"So did I. But he's definitely homegrown."

"So where is he, then?"

"Sidmouth."

Angus knew the town. It was a Regency seaside town east of Exeter. "Great. I know Sidmouth well; I've been to the folk festival every year since I was ten."

Charlotte smirked. "You like folk music?"

Angus raised his eyebrows. "Why is that amusing? I have Scottish parents, remember, and besides, it's a fabulous melting pot of music, dance and storytelling from all over the world. You should try it – you might like it."

"Is that a challenge?"

Angus considered. "I suppose it is. It's not long till the festival; why don't you come with me? For a concert, or just to walk around the town. They have lots of street performers."

"Okay, why not," said Charlotte. "Misty told me to try new things." Misty was Charlotte's therapist and had proved invaluable before, during and after her divorce. But she did pay her obscene amounts of money to be available to her twenty-four seven.

"Shall we go now and see what he's up to?"

Charlotte smiled. "That's why I came; I thought we could go straight there. Is that okay?"

"Sure." Angus started the engine and they set off. "So, how did you find out where the catfisher lived?" he asked. "Without too much technobabble, please."

"It was the photos. Every digital photo has information embedded in it: the GPS location of where it was taken, the date and time, the camera used, and even the lens of the camera."

"I knew about the GPS, but not the other things."

"The catfisher sent Katrina lots of photos of someone who he said was him, and some pictures of his house and dog. Most of the pictures were stolen, but the ones of his house and dog were real."

Angus glanced at Charlotte. "Wouldn't he know that info was there, though? If he set up a catfishing scam, he must be a bit tech-savvy?"

"Yes, but he made one mistake. On one of the photos, he'd forgotten to remove the hidden data. His house is on the outskirts of the town, so it was easy to pinpoint."

Angus glanced at her again and smiled. "Good work."

It took them half an hour to get to Sidmouth. Charlotte directed Angus to the address and he stopped the car a short distance away.

His house was on a quiet cul-de-sac on the outskirts of

Exe Factor

the town. There were five bungalows all with well-mani-
cured front lawns, and set back from the road. Angus had
barely switched the engine off before Charlotte got out her
laptop and started scanning for his Wi-Fi. He glanced at the
screen, saw the computer code and looked away. He felt his
shoulders tense. How she actually liked all that, he'd never
know.

A few minutes later, she muttered, "I'm in. His Wi-Fi
password was hard to crack, but I got there in the end."

"I never doubted you for a minute," Angus mused.

Charlotte typed at lightning speed. "Let's see what he's
doing. I'll download and monitor some data to see what he's
been up to on the internet." She thought about leaving
malware on his computer to track it even more closely, but
she'd have to gather the data. That was too risky; it would be
too easy to track her. For a moment she thought about the
possible consequences of her actions. What she was doing
was totally illegal, but this man was a scammer and a thief.
If helping her friend meant breaking a few laws, it was
worth it.

Not that she would get caught. Charlotte knew how to
hide her illicit activity. She was using a VPN – a virtual
private network – an encrypted link, and a Kali Linux oper-
ating system, which all made her impossible to track.

Her concentration on the task was broken by Angus
typing on his phone. "The name of the man who lives at this
address is Robert Hubbard," he announced.

Charlotte looked up, impressed. "How did you find
out?"

"I may be a technophobe, but I also subscribe to a
website which holds this sort of info, mainly from the electoral register."

"Using websites doesn't count as tech."

"Not to you. But I am using a computer – even if it's a smartphone computer."

"True," she conceded.

"Looks like he's been living here about a year."

A small van passed them and parked at the house. The driver left the engine running, took a parcel from the boot and knocked on the door.

The door opened. Angus reached for his phone and took photos of Robert Hubbard. He was wearing jeans, a black T-shirt and a black baseball cap that shaded most of his face.

"From what little I can see, he's younger than I thought," Charlotte commented. "Vile piece of shit. I bet he's renting that house using money he's scammed from innocent women like Katrina. It makes my blood boil."

"Don't hold back, Charlotte," Angus commented, with amusement in his voice.

"I won't! He's caused horrible pain to my friend Katrina and he doesn't give a shit about her. I bet there are other victims, and I want to know how many." She smiled an evil smile. "I bet a lot of people would like to know exactly where he lives."

Angus stared at her. "If you tell everybody where he is, Charlotte, he'll just do a runner. Better to figure out who his victims are and take the evidence to the police, and they will deal with him."

Charlotte stared back, then huffed a sigh. He was right, of course. He was always right when it came to things like this, which was infuriating. Her therapist, Misty, kept telling her to stop letting her heart rule her head. That was nice, in theory, but when it came to ripping off her friends, Charlotte had little sympathy for anyone.

"I'm going to get as much evidence as I can. This might take some time."

Angus shrugged. "Why don't you come back with Grigore and spend some time looking into what he's doing. If you need me to help, just call me."

"All right."

"We can stay a bit longer, though. He might go out," he said.

As luck would have it, Hubbard did go out about half an hour later, with a small dog on a lead: the one from the photos he'd sent Katrina. He wore the same clothes, including the baseball cap. The dog, an overexcited long-haired Chihuahua, pulled him along. He didn't notice Charlotte and Angus because he was glued to a smart-phone. He walked down the road and disappeared around the corner.

"Should we follow him by foot?" Charlotte asked.

"I think we should. Do you need to stay here and get more info off his computer?"

Charlotte nodded. "I can sniff around more if he's not there."

"I'll follow him. I suspect he's just walking the dog, but you never know. I'll keep you updated."

Angus got out the car and disappeared around the corner. About ten minutes later, Charlotte got a text: *He's on his way back.*

She'd done all she could on his Wi-Fi, so she closed her laptop and waited for Hubbard to reappear. Five minutes later, he came around the corner, this time not staring at his phone. Charlotte picked up her phone and pretended to speak to someone, but he went inside without looking at her.

A couple of minutes later, Angus got into the car. "Was he up to anything exciting?" Charlotte asked.

"No, he was buried in his phone, so there was no risk of him seeing me. He walked for about ten minutes until he got to a small park. He let the dog off the lead and sat on one of the benches, still looking at his phone."

Charlotte smiled. "What?" Angus asked.

"You can take the man out of the police, but you can't take the police out of the man. You still report just like a detective."

Angus frowned, then looked at her closed laptop. "You say it like it's a bad thing."

Charlotte frowned. "I didn't mean it in a bad way. It's endearing."

"I take it you're done?"

"Yep. I need to do a full analysis of the data I copied, but I need my home computer for that."

Angus started the car and they drove back to Exeter.

"How long do you think it will take for you finish the work on Mr Perry?"

Angus glanced at her. "I'm not sure. What I am sure of is he's making a false claim; I just needed to prove it. Mr Perry has admitted he was in financial trouble, which makes me even more suspicious. And it was odd that specific items such as antique cameras were the only items stolen."

"Who would have targeted those?"

Angus frowned. "Not many people would be interested enough in old-style photography to want to rob him."

"His house was large and grand, and despite having a certain shabbiness, there were definitely more valuable items for opportunist burglars to steal."

"Yep, most burglars would take anything they could sell on quickly; they're often drug addicts needing money for their next fix. They'd take TVs or other electrical equipment, not antique cameras. I'd bet large sums of money he has the items stashed somewhere; I just have to find out where."

"Isn't there some sort of police department that deals with this type of case?" Charlotte asked.

"Yes, The Insurance Fraud Enforcement Department; there's one in every constabulary. I never had much to do with the one in the Devon and Cornwall Police."

"The fact that you're investigating it means Mr Perry might shift the 'stolen' items somewhere. We could watch him."

Angus shook his head. "We're not being paid to do that."

Chapter Five

Angus dropped Charlotte in Topsham and went home to start his report on Mr Perry's insurance claim.

His house was a semi in the Pennsylvania area of Exeter; the quiet suburban street suited him now that he was in his early fifties. He'd grown up in Exeter and he never wanted to leave, even though his Scottish parents and wider family had tried to get him to move to Scotland multiple times.

After he'd made himself a stir-fry for dinner, he opened a beer and took out his notebook. He started writing his report, and decided he should also speak to Mrs Carter, the elderly woman who had answered the door. It would be tricky, since she was as deaf as a doorpost, but he had bags of patience when it came to the elderly. He'd interview her in her own home, though.

The next morning, he went for a 10K run. When he got back, he found a text from Charlotte. That wasn't unusual. She'd got into the habit of texting him most mornings since they had been working together: sometimes about nothing, sometimes something important. He liked it, though. She was a smart woman, and he liked having someone to talk to about work. When he'd started his private investigation business after leaving the police, he hadn't realised how much he'd miss working with someone else.

Come over when you're ready. Have full info on what Robert Hubbard has been up to.

Angus hit Reply. *Will be over in an hour, just got back from run.*

When he reached Charlotte's house just over an hour later, there was another car in the driveway: a white Fiat.

Helena opened the door, beaming. "Mr Angus!" She always seemed pleased to see him. "Charlotte, she in office." She indicated the way and closed the door behind him.

He went through the house and found Charlotte behind her huge mahogany desk, with another woman sitting opposite her.

Charlotte stood up. "Angus, this is my friend Katrina. Katrina, this is Angus. He's the man I told you about the other day, the one I've been working with."

Angus held out his hand to shake Katrina's, then wondered if he should have. With men he always shook hands, but with women he wasn't sure if that was what you did these days. She took it with a fleeting smile. Then he sat down in the vacant chair next to her.

"I asked Katrina over so that I could tell you both what I've found out about Mr Hubbard and his antics. It isn't pretty."

Angus nodded.

Katrina wriggled in her seat and fluttered her eyelashes at Angus. "You must think me an absolute idiot, falling for such a scam."

Angus shook his head. "I've never blamed a victim for

any crime. None of this is your fault. It can happen to anyone."

Katrina looked down at her hands.

Charlotte coughed and they both looked at her. "So, I spent yesterday afternoon and evening analysing the data. I knew that all the stuff I found couldn't be used as evidence, because of the way I obtained it, but I could at least find out if there were other victims. It didn't take me long to find them: he has eleven people on the go. I'm not sure how he manages it all, to be honest, but I've no doubt there have been plenty of others. He was using a different profile for each one; I have no idea how he doesn't get confused."

Angus listened, silent.

"His fake profiles were of women when he was targeting men, and vice versa. No wonder he was glued to his phone when he took his dog for a walk: he was probably messaging his victims. It must take him all day, every day."

Charlotte looked over her laptop at them, then turned it to show them the screen.

"This is Robert Hubbard. He's been living at that address for over six months. He doesn't seem to be from Devon, and he wasn't registered in the area before then. I suspect Robert Hubbard isn't his real name either."

She tapped the keyboard, and the screen changed to show one of the photos they'd taken of him the day before, his face barely visible beneath the baseball cap. "Looking at the files on his computer, he's up to all sorts of other things too. He's installed the TOR browser, which is deeply suspicious."

Angus sighed. "Charlotte, please remember that when you talk about computers, you need to explain it to me. I have no idea what you're talking about with this 'taw' browser."

Katrina giggled. "She's terrible, isn't she? She's always done the same to me too. I never have a clue what she's talking about."

Charlotte's eyes narrowed ever so slightly as she looked at Katrina. Then she turned to Angus. "A TOR browser is how you access the dark Web. TOR stands for 'The Onion Router', because of the way it hides your identity and lets you access the darker side of the internet. It's not illegal to have it, and not everyone who uses it does illegal things, but seeing as he's a nasty catfisher, it's fair to guess he's been up to no good with it."

Angus nodded. "I agree." Before he left the police, he had been involved with numerous cases where criminals were using the dark Web, usually to launder money or sell drugs.

"What he was doing on there was tricky to find out, because there was no website history, whereas the everyday browsers most people use keep a history of the sites visited. I did find a number of different files that indicated he was doing something with cryptocurrencies."

Angus leaned forward. "What sort of activities?"

"Possibly money laundering, maybe drugs money. It's very complex, but I think he takes money from his handler and buys local cryptocurrencies."

Katrina, who had been sitting in silence, spoke up. "Local cryptocurrencies? Is there no end to the tech stuff out there? What on earth are those?"

"It's where local vendors give you Bitcoin or other cryptocurrencies in exchange for cash. It's used by anyone who wants to launder money, because it's all under the radar."

"So he's an organised criminal and he needs reporting," Katrina said, and sat back.

"How do we report this to the police?" Charlotte asked

Angus. "Is this something Katrina has to do?" She paused. "I mean, I can tell Mark, but he'll probably go ballistic when he knows what I've been doing." She tapped the keyboard.

Angus nodded. "The victim needs to report it, really. The police will take it more seriously, then."

They were interrupted by Helena coming in with a tray of coffees. "Here you go," she said as she set the tray down on the desk.

"Thank you, darling." Charlotte helped Helena distribute the cups. Angus had been to Charlotte's home so many times now that Helena knew how he took his coffee.

Helena looked at the screen, where Robert Hubbard was still displayed. "Horrible man, is there no end to it? What police do? In Romania, men like this sorted out – no police." She drew her finger across her throat.

"As tempting as that sounds, it's not an option here," said Angus, with a slight smile.

Helena snorted. "Zometimes things need sort – no police."

"Don't worry, he's been up to all sorts of things – he won't get away with it," Charlotte replied.

Helena harrumphed, and left the room.

Katrina leaned forward, fluttered her eyelashes and crossed her legs at Angus. "I do hope you're right, Charlotte. It's awful to have been victimised like this. I just hope he doesn't do it to anyone else."

Charlotte grew more and more exasperated with Katrina as time went on. The moment Angus had entered the room, she'd transformed from sad and deflated to eyelash-fluttering and demure. Goodness, how she hated women who changed the moment a man walked into the room. Why had she never seen that before? She clearly fancies Angus, she thought, and felt a stab of jealousy. What if Angus liked her back?

Charlotte took a sip of coffee to calm herself down. "I'll collect the evidence, and you can take it to the police."

"Thank you, darling," said Katrina. "Although, it would mean the world to me if I didn't have to go there all alone."

"Would you come with me?" Katrina asked.

It took a while for Angus, who had been looking at the laptop screen, to register the deathly silence. He looked from Katrina to Charlotte, and hesitated. "Wouldn't you prefer Charlotte?"

Charlotte looked away.

Katrina shook her head. "Charlotte's done more than enough for me already. I wouldn't like to impose on her."

Charlotte turned back to Angus with what he privately called *that look* on her face. The one that said, *Make the right decision, or else.* Except he wasn't sure what the right decision was.

"Oh, I'm happy to go with you," said Charlotte, "but we can't mention that I obtained the evidence, or how I did it."

Katrina smirked. "Angus has been in the police, and he'll know exactly what to say." She looked at him with big, adoring eyes.

Charlotte's mouth fell open. Then she looked at Angus, who seemed completely oblivious.

She raised her eyebrows. "Don't be silly, Katrina. I'll take you. Angus is very busy with the case he's working on at the moment, aren't you?" She didn't wait for him to respond, which was rather rude, but she didn't care. "Phone them today and make an appointment to report a crime."

Katrina pouted.

Charlotte turned the laptop back round and started typing. "I'll get the evidence together now."

Angus drained his cup and stood up. "I'd better get on with that report, and I've got to interview a few more people too. By the way, that juju you did with Robert Hubbard's photos. Can you do the same with the photos Mr Perry took of his stolen cameras, and tell me where and when they were taken?"

Charlotte looked over her laptop at him. "Of course. Email them over and I'll give you a full analysis."

"Thanks." He turned to Katrina. "It was nice to meet you."

Katrina blinked up at him. "You too."

Both women watched Angus leave. As soon as the front door closed, Katrina leaned back in her chair. "Oh my God, Charlotte, he is div-ine! Why didn't you tell me how lovely he is?"

Charlotte stopped typing again and looked at Katrina. A million thoughts went through her mind. Of course Katrina would find Angus attractive. She did too. He was also honourable and caring. It was a minor miracle that he hadn't already been snapped up by some woman when his marriage broke up.

A surge of jealousy went through Charlotte, followed by guilt. What was she doing, getting annoyed at her friend? She loved Katrina, and she couldn't let a man come between them. But she was not going to encourage them in any way.

Angus isn't interested in me, anyway, she thought with some bitterness. After all, he'd turned her down when she'd made a drunken pass at him.

"Yes, Angus is a lovely man." Maybe changing the subject was the best idea. "Are you staying for lunch?"

Katrina stood up. "I'd better get back. I need to put in extra hours now to make up the money I lost. We're short-staffed at the moment anyway." Katrina was veterinary nurse now. She'd retrained a few years back after decades of various managerial jobs in insurance or finance companies.

Charlotte sighed. "Let me give it to you, darling. I've just had a massive payout from an investment." The saying that "Money makes money" was true.

"No, it was my fault, and I need to live with the consequences. But thank you for offering."

Charlotte pressed a button and the printer beside her started up.

Katrina left with the evidence: Robert Hubbard's GPS location from the photos, his address, a printout of the messages between them and a list of people he was currently catfishing. Hopefully the police would be on the case quickly.

Chapter Six

The next morning, Angus had a phone call from Charlotte while he was lying under a bathroom sink in one of the flats he rented out. He took the call, and she didn't wait for him to speak. "Where are you? I've looked at Mr Perry's photos and sent you a full report on them. Have you seen it?"

"I'm in the flats; there's a leaky pipe in one of the bathrooms."

"Are you fixing it yourself?"

"I am. They're usually easy to sort out. Just a leak in a joint on the incoming cold tap."

Charlotte was silent for a moment. "Well, anyway, all the photos have GPS information and dates. And you were right; he's lying about the cameras. The photos were all taken at an address in Ireland, a week after he said the burglary took place."

Angus sat up. "I knew it. What's the location in Ireland?"

"I've looked it up, and it's a farmhouse in the middle of

nowhere. I checked the Irish land-registry website, did a little digging and it belongs to his cousin."

"Keeping it in the family," Angus commented. "And you've already emailed me the info?"

"Of course. Look, Angus, I want to go and watch Robert Hubbard again, and see if he's been up to anything else. I left a program running on his computer that collected data from his dark Web use."

"Why do you have to go there? Isn't it being beamed across the internet to you?"

"Nope, despite being an expert at hiding my tracks, I wanted to make doubly sure, so I just got the program to store the data on his computer."

"Want me to come?"

"Would you? From the data I got last time, he's meeting a dealer, or someone who could be a dealer, at four pm. You're better at the covert stuff. It's at his house."

"I'll pick you up at three."

At three thirty, they reached Robert Hubbard's house. Angus parked the car in a different place, but in any case, his black VW Golf was pretty inconspicuous. He'd chosen it for just that reason.

Charlotte got out her laptop and pressed a few keys. "Hopefully he hasn't spotted my little program. It was designed to be inconspicuous if he went snooping around his computer files." She frowned. "Hang on, that's strange. His Wi-Fi isn't on the list. Maybe we're too far away. I need to get closer."

"You need to wait." Angus indicated a car that had just passed them. The Volvo estate parked on Hubbard's driveway. Angus made a note of the number plate, in his notebook. A man in his mid twenties got out and knocked on the door. They could see the dog through the frosted glass of the door, jumping up and barking.

A minute later, the man knocked again, but the door remained closed. He shouted through the letterbox, which made the dog go berserk. Then he took out his phone.

"No doubt he's calling Hubbard," said Angus. "And by the looks of it, he's not answering that either."

After a few minutes, the man got in his car and left.

"If he's not in, I can have another look at his Wi-Fi," said Charlotte. "He might be using a different frequency."

Angus nodded, then reached behind him to the back seat and pulled out two high-vis yellow jackets and two clipboards with blank paper on them. "Put this on. Nobody questions anyone with a high-vis jacket."

Charlotte's eyes widened. "Really?"

"Yep. You can get away with all sorts of things."

She held up the jacket, on the back of which was written "DFR Survey". "What's a DFR survey?"

"Whatever you like. You change it depending on the situation you find yourself in. Driving Federation Research, Digital Federation Consumables, D—"

"All right, I get the idea. Let's have a look."

They got out of the car and put on the jackets, then walked to Hubbard's house. Charlotte walked partway round the house, out of view of the neighbours, and opened her laptop. Angus stood nearby and watched for Hubbard.

"I still can't find his Wi-Fi." She slammed her laptop shut and Angus came over. "Let's have a quick look round the back. We may be able to see in through a window. Maybe he'll have papers lying around."

Charlotte followed Angus. The gate that led to the back of the house was unlocked, and they walked through. The garden was large and manicured, with trees around the edge. There was a patio next to the house, with a table and four chairs.

Angus went to the first window and looked through, cupping his hand around his eyes. "Kitchen," he said. "A few dirty plates and cups in the sink, but nothing else."

Charlotte joined him, and looked in too. "Cleaner than I thought it would be."

Angus went to the next window, a sliding patio door. He looked in, then took a step back. Charlotte was still looking through the kitchen window when he turned to her. "That explains why he wasn't answering the door..."

"What is it?" Charlotte walked over. It took a moment for her to register what she saw. A man's body slumped on the floor. Then she gasped. "Oh my God, he's dead!"

Chapter Seven

Charlotte was frozen to the spot for a moment. Then she turned to Angus. "How ... who?"

Angus shrugged to give himself time. It could be anyone, but they knew one obvious suspect with a very good motive: Katrina.

"Is he actually dead?" Charlotte looked briefly in the window.

"His eyes are open and still, and there is a knife in his chest. I'm pretty sure." He took out his mobile phone, opened his contacts list, then glanced at Charlotte and put it away. "Are you all right?" he asked, scrutinising her.

Charlotte swallowed. "No, I don't think I am," she gasped.

"You're as white as a sheet. Come and sit down over here while I call the police." He led her over to the table and she sat down, staring straight in front of her. "Is that your first dead body?"

She nodded.

He bent down, a concerned look on his face. "Don't look again. Stay here, and I'll deal with it."

She nodded again.

He walked away from the table, took out his phone and dialled. "Woody, it's Angus." He took a blue latex glove from his pocket, put it on and tried the patio door. It was open.

Charlotte watched him disappear into the house, then heard the yapping of a dog. Hubbard's dog.

A few moments later, Angus reappeared, phone in one hand and dog in the other. The dog had stopped yapping and was shaking, looking up at Angus with big brown eyes. "Look after this, will you?" He handed her the dog and went back in.

"Hello..." Charlotte cooed. "I don't normally like dogs, but you're cute." She held the dog up. Its ears were back and it was still shaking. She put the long-haired Chihuahua on her lap. "There's no need to shake. I'm not going to hurt you, little one."

The dog still stared at her as she stroked it, and after a minute it stopped shaking.

She could hear the distant sound of Angus's voice as he spoke to her brother. Then there was silence, and he came outside. "He's definitely dead. Rigor mortis has already set in. The knife looks like it might be from the kitchen." He crouched down so that his eyes were level with Charlotte's. "Are you okay?"

The dog growled, and he stared at it. "Is that rat behaving itself?"

Charlotte hugged the dog. "He's not a rat!"

Angus stood up. "That's a matter of opinion. The police are on their way. More specifically, your brother. He'll be here in about twenty minutes, and he's asked us not to pollute the crime scene. Including the garden. The patio door was open, so there might be evidence out here."

Charlotte looked up at Angus. "Who would want to kill him?"

"Judging by what you described yesterday, a lot of people. If he's involved in drugs or money laundering, which is a definite possibility, he could well have annoyed someone."

"We're the only ones who knew he was catfishing. And neither of us did it."

Angus studied her. "Katrina knew too."

"Katrina would never hurt anyone."

Angus raised his eyebrows. "The families and close friends of murderers rarely thought their loved ones were capable of killing. He was involved in a lot of dodgy stuff. Statistically, it's likely to be one of his associates."

Charlotte nodded. "I suppose getting access to his computer is out of the question?"

"You'd have to go through the house, past his body and you'd leave your DNA everywhere."

She blinked at him. "What if I was chasing after a dog?"

Angus sighed. "No. You might destroy vital clues. You could ask your brother; he might give you access."

The dog started to growl at Angus, who gave it a side-long glance.

Charlotte stroked its head. "It's okay, darling. Uncle Angus won't hurt you. There, there. You're very sweet. I wonder what your name is?"

"Ratty," muttered Angus.

It took Charlotte's brother, DCI Mark Lockwood, or Woody to almost everyone else, twenty minutes to arrive.

He pulled up outside the house in an unmarked car. Charlotte was waiting for him with the dog. Angus had remained in the back garden, because every time he went near the dog, it growled.

Woody got out of the car. He was in a dark suit, no tie. Charlotte lifted herself up on her toes and kissed her brother on the cheek. "Thank goodness you're here."

"What have you been up to, sis, discovering a dead body?"

The dog wriggled in her arms. "I didn't know you'd got a dog." Woody bent down to look. "Hello, little fella." The dog yapped at him. "That's not very nice."

Charlotte held the wriggling dog tighter. "It's all right, little one. Mark won't hurt you either." She looked up at her brother. "It seems to have a problem with men."

Mark shook his head as Angus came round the corner of the house and approached them. "Woody." The men shook hands. Then another man got out of Woody's car. He was young, and Angus realised he didn't know him.

"This is DS Spencer," said Woody. "Gary, this is Angus Darrow, formerly Inspector Darrow and my little sister, Charlie, so be nice." Woody took blue latex gloves from his jacket pocket and put them on.

Charlotte's eyes narrowed. "It's Charlotte, by the way, not Charlie."

DS Spencer nodded to them both.

Woody flexed his fingers in the gloves. "SOCO will be here soon. In the meantime, let's have a look, shall we?"

Angus led them around the side of the house to the patio door. Charlotte followed, but stayed on the patio. "If you see a dog lead in there, can you bring it out?" she asked. "Then I can keep the dog under control."

Angus nodded and went into the house behind Woody and DS Spencer.

Robert Hubbard's body was sprawled across the lounge

floor, half on its side. Woody and Spencer knelt and examined it.

Angus stood on the other side of the body. "I'm no expert, but I reckon he was killed last night."

Woody touched the corpse's arm. "Yeah, he's cold and stiff. I reckon he's been dead for some time." He peered at the body a while, then sighed and stood up. "Let's have a look around, then ... Spencer, you go upstairs. Angus and I will check things out down here."

Spencer nodded, then left the room and they heard the stairs creak.

"So, what were you two doing here?" Woody asked.

"Investigating this guy. He catfished Charlotte's friend."

"Really? Naughty boy, then, are we?" Woody said to the body. "No prizes for guessing how Charlie found out where he lived..."

Angus nodded. "My lips are sealed."

"Hello? Are you there?" Charlotte was outside the patio door, standing with her back to them. "Have you found a lead? The dog is getting fractious."

"He's her first dead body," said Angus.

"Really? Yeah, I suppose he is. Wish I'd got to nearly fifty without seeing one," said Woody.

Angus chuckled. "Shouldn't have joined the police, then."

Woody moved silently to the door until he was standing close to Charlotte's back. "Charlie," he said, at his normal volume.

Charlotte screamed. The dog jumped out of her arms, then ran into the house.

"Oh my goodness, Mark, why did you do that?" She turned round and whacked him on the arm.

"Ow!" he cried, rubbing his arm and smirking. "You

shouldn't let a simple thing like a dead body spook you, sis. It can't hurt you."

Charlotte remembered the body, and looked horrified. The dog sniffed around the body, then sat next to it. "Shouldn't we keep the dog away?" Charlotte asked, briefly peering around Woody.

Angus went over to the dog and picked it up. This time it didn't growl. He left the room, and returned a minute later with the dog on a lead. He handed it to Charlotte, who was still outside.

Ten minutes later, more police and the SOCO team arrived and got to work. Woody came out of the house not long afterwards. "I'll send a uniform to take your statements, but you can go for now."

"What about the dog?" Charlotte asked, looking down. The dog was asleep on her lap.

"Why don't you take it home for now?" said Woody. "It seems to like you."

She hesitated for a moment. "Me? All right."

Angus frowned. He wasn't keen on small dogs, and that one would be in his car for at least half an hour. He hoped it wouldn't pee on the seat.

Luckily, the journey to Topsham was uneventful.

Charlotte had messaged Helena to buy some dog food, but when Helena saw the dog, she scoffed. "Most cat bigger than zis thing. In Romania many strays and they would eat it."

Angus had followed Charlotte and the dog in, and smiled at Helena's comment.

Charlotte's mouth dropped open. "How awful!" She

stroked the dog's head. "I'll protect you from nasty big doggies..."

"What name?"

"I have no idea, but I'll go through the data I got off the catfisher's computer and see if I can find out."

Angus went with Charlotte to the office. "I'll check the photos I took in his house."

"What did you take photos of?"

"Just all around. There wasn't much of interest. By the way the house was decorated, I'd guess he rented it furnished." Angus bent his neck to study one of the photos, then used his fingers to zoom in.

Their silent working was interrupted by a crash from the kitchen, followed by the sound of yapping. Helena came in, scowling. "That dog, it zo small I no see it. It no leave me alone. Charlotte, I look after you and house, but not dog. No." She made a cross sign with her arms.

"He's probably hungry and scared." Charlotte stood up and left the room. She returned a few moments later carrying the dog. "Angus and Helena, meet Elvis."

"Elvis?" Angus and Helena said, in the same surprised tone.

"Yep, Elvis. I found an email to his vet."

"Zat stupid name for dog. Elvis vaz big strong man. Dog iz small and annoying." Helena tossed her head and walked out of the room.

Charlotte carried Elvis into the kitchen. "Don't you worry about Helena," she cooed to him. "Her bark is worse than her bite."

She put him down, took out a tin of food and emptied it into the empty bowl on the floor. He started eating so she left him to it.

She went back into the office to find Angus on the phone.

From what he was saying, she worked out he was speaking to her brother. When he ended the call, he put his phone on the table. "That was Woody. They are treating it as murder and have a number of possible suspects already."

"That's fast. Did he say who they were?"

"No. But you can be sure he'll look into Katrina."

Charlotte scowled. "Well, I suppose he has to rule her out."

Chapter Eight

The next morning, Charlotte got a text from her brother:

Sending uniform to Angus's house to take your statements. 10am.

Charlotte grimaced at his assumption she would just go. Well, of course she would, but it was still a bit of cheek that he didn't check she was busy. She took Elvis out for a short walk first, then fed him. She dithered whether to leave him in the house, but in the end decided to take him with her in the hope he would get used to Angus.

When she got there, a police car was parked outside on the road, indicating the officer had already arrived. She knocked on his front door, Elvis in her arms. When Angus saw the dog, he shook his head. "That rat is not coming in here."

"He's not a rat! Poor Elvie baby, Uncle Angus is not usually this mean, you know." She stroked his head and stared at Angus. "He's normally lovely. Grigore has to leave, and he won't look after him..."

Angus sighed. "You can leave him in the garage."

Charlotte paused for a moment, then remembered Angus's garage had a carpet and was as neat and tidy as the rest of his house. "All right."

He beckoned her in and she went through. He opened the door to the garage and she took Elvis inside. Angus switched on the light, and got the dog an old rug to sit on. Charlotte put him down on it, and petted him for a moment. "I'll come and see you later." Elvis looked up at her with expectant wide eyes and she gave him a doggy treat.

They went through to the living room to find the officer: a petite woman, dark brown hair tied back in a bun, aged about thirty in full uniform sat with an A4 folder in one hand and a cup of tea in the other. "PC Sophia Wright." She didn't stand up. "You must be Miss Lockwood. DCI Lockwood's sister?"

"I am."

"You don't look much like him," PC Wright said, staring at her for a moment. Charlotte sat in the chair opposite her.

"Thank goodness for that!" Charlotte stated dryly.

"Tea?" Angus asked. There was a collection of tea things on a side table.

She nodded. Charlotte wasn't in the mood to sit and give a statement. She could think of a hundred different things she could be doing instead of this. Statements always took so long.

There was an awkward silence as Angus poured the tea, then handed the mug to her.

"So..." PC Wright put her cup down. "Shall we start from the beginning?" She opened her folder and took out a pen. "You discovered the body?"

"I saw it first," Angus stated. "Through the window of the back door."

PC Wright started to write down notes. "And why were you there?"

Angus and Charlotte looked at each other. Angus gave a small nod to Charlotte so she spoke: "We're private investigators."

"And you were investigating Robert Hubbard?"

"Yes."

"What for?"

Charlotte glanced at Angus again. The look on his face said, *Tell the truth.* Well, she couldn't tell all the truth about how she found him and tried to hack into his computer.

"Catfishing."

PC Wright nodded and wrote some more notes. Charlotte realised now why Angus wrote everything in his notebook too. It was clearly mandatory on the first day of training in the police and was a hard habit to break.

Nearly an hour later, the statement was done, and PC Wright left. Angus came back into the living room after seeing her out.

"How did you not die of boredom doing things like that?" Charlotte asked him. "No wonder you left the police. If that's what you had to do all the time."

Angus started clearing away the tea things. "That's what the junior officers are for."

They headed out to walk Elvis in a nearby park.

"I've been reading up about caring for Chihuahuas. Although they're small, they still need plenty of exercise."

"I'll take your word for it," said Angus. "I've never liked dogs much; I prefer cats. I also prefer dogs that are bigger than cats."

Charlotte ignored the comment and gestured towards the bench. "Has my brother told you any more about what they found?"

"A little. As we know, he was stabbed, and the time of death was around three am that night."

"Three am? That's unusual, isn't it?"

Angus leaned back on the bench. "Not really. I don't think there's a usual time for murder; they just happen when the murderer decides to murder."

Charlotte gave him a sidewise glance. "I mean, who would have visited him at that time of night? Someone up to no good. I bet you're right and it's a gang member he was working with. As soon as I get home, I'll have another look at that data. It's annoying I couldn't get any more."

They sat side by side, silent. "Does it get any easier?" Charlotte asked. "You know. The more dead bodies you see, does it get easier to be around them?"

Angus considered, then looked at her. "A bit, although it's always strange. I've not seen as many as some of my colleagues. Most weren't murder victims, though. They were in their homes and died of natural causes."

"I could never work in a job where there was the remotest possibility of a dead body turning up."

Angus's mouth curved to a smile. "You're already in a job where a dead body has turned up. More than once."

Charlotte grimaced. Angus meant Billy, the uncle of Daniel, a boy who had disappeared. Tracking down Daniel had been their first case together. "I didn't see Billy's body, though." That was the night she'd got drunk and made a pass at Angus. They'd talked about *that* kiss briefly the next day, but neither had mentioned it since. Charlotte could barely remember it due to the amount of alcohol she'd consumed. He'd not hinted why he'd turned down a night of sex.

"'There's not much we can do now; your brother and the rest of Devon and Cornwall Police can deal with it. We've got plenty of insurance fraud cases we could take on if we wanted to."

"You're right. I'll phone Katrina and tell her."

Charlotte pulled out her phone, handed Elvis's lead to Angus, stood up and walked away from the bench. A few minutes later, she came back and sat down. "Katrina was shocked, but she didn't seem too upset."

"I'm not surprised. He stole her life savings."

"Do you think she'll get her money back?" asked Charlotte.

"It depends whether he'd spent the money. Even if he hadn't, no doubt other people he scammed will want some of it."

"Have you found anything interesting in the photos?"

"Not yet. I'll send them over and you can have a look." She nodded.

He stood up. "I need to go; I have a training session. I need to run 15K if I'm going to stay on schedule."

"See you tomorrow, then?"

He smiled, then left.

When Angus got home he messaged his friend Graham, who was an equally keen runner, to check he was still coming. They'd been training together after committing to run the Grizzly, and had planned their training in detail, allowing a contingency for illness or work commitments.

They met at Haldon Forest, a popular spot a few miles outside the city. It had circular paths for walkers, runners and cyclists, and they planned to run the 15K cycle track that circled the forest boundary.

Angus was first to arrive, and waited in his car until he saw Graham pull up. He got out and went over to him.

Graham was a few years older than Angus. He was stocky and wouldn't have looked out of place on the rugby field.

"You ready for this?" Graham asked as he got out his car. He was already in his running gear: shorts and running top. The men shook hands.

"Absolutely," Angus replied. "Been looking forward to it."

They locked their cars, counted down, started their GPS watches and set off. The plan was to warm up, and then run at a good steady pace and aim for a time under one hour forty-five minutes.

Being mid-week, the forest was quiet despite the weather being clear and bright. The forest was at a higher altitude than Exeter, so it could often be windy, but not today.

"How's work been?" Graham asked, as they rounded a bend.

"Oh, you know, steady. Much less stressful than the police. Can't complain. You?"

Graham managed a distribution depot for a major supermarket. The hours were long and the work stressful. They'd known each other near five years when they'd regularly attended the 5K parkrun every Saturday morning at Exeter Quay and got talking. "Same as ever. Wish I had the guts to do an Angus and go it alone."

Angus smiled. "You know I'd advise everyone to do it. Being your own COE – chief of everything – has many advantages."

A few kilometres in, they reached a narrow, uneven part of the track, which descended sharply.

Angus took the lead, slowing down to negotiate the bumps and loose stones. A few seconds later, he heard a yell behind him, and the sound of gravel skittering. He came carefully to a stop and looked round. Graham was lying on the floor, white as a sheet, clutching his ankle.

Angus's phone rang and he winced. He was in the waiting room of the A&E Department at Exeter Hospital, sitting directly opposite a No Mobile Phones sign. It was a stupid rule; everyone had a mobile phone these days. It ought to say no filming or photographs. For a moment he thought about going outside, but stopped himself.

The waiting room was full of people. One man was clutching his arm, while another had his leg elevated on the chair next to him. On the other side of the room was a mother with her daughter about eight or nine years old, who, every so often, vomited into a bag. *How I hate hospitals.*

He looked at the phone, then the sign, then shrugged and answered. "Charlotte, why are you calling this late?"

It was late: past eight o'clock. He was tired and fed up, but somehow the sound of her voice was soothing. Earlier, when Graham had fallen over, he'd phoned for an ambulance, but it had taken them nearly an hour to arrive, and he hadn't been allowed to travel in the ambulance with Graham because he wasn't family. He'd gone home, showered and changed, and was now back at the hospital, waiting for news. Graham's wife was in with him, but he still felt guilty, even though it wasn't his fault.

"Are you okay?" asked Charlotte. She sounded worried.

"Yeah, why?"

"You're in A&E. Are you hurt?"

"No, it's my friend Graham. He broke his leg when we were out running. Well, we think it's broken."

"How awful. But you're okay?"

He sighed. "I'm fine. Anyway, how do you know I'm in A&E?"

It was a rhetorical question; he knew how. She had that tracking app, the one you can use to find your friends. He had friends who used it to track their elderly relatives, and he guessed that some people used it to track their partners and see what they were up to. He didn't remember giving her permission to track him on it. In fact, he knew he hadn't.

"Oh, you know..." she mumbled. "Oh, hi, Helena. Got to go, Angus. Glad you're okay. Give my regards to Gary."

"It's Graham," he corrected.

But the line had already gone dead.

Angus sighed again and rubbed his forehead. He was being tracked – or was it stalked? He wasn't sure whether he should feel annoyed or pleased. It certainly explained why she kept turning up wherever he was, and how she had known he was at Exeter Hospital.

He swiped through his home screen to find the app. What was it called again? There were too many apps on his phone; he needed to get rid of all the ones he never used.

He was in the process of deleting some, when a nurse called his name. He stood up and went over to her. "Mr Darrow? Your friend has broken his ankle. It's quite a bad fracture, and they need to put some plates and screws in, so they'll operate in the morning. He should make a full recovery, though."

"Can I see him?"

"That probably isn't a good idea. He's been given morphine for the pain, so you won't get much sense out of him. Anyway, his wife is with him."

That made Angus feel better. "All right, thanks. I'll come back tomorrow. When are visiting hours?"

"Two pm to eight pm. You can just turn up." She smiled.

Angus nodded. "Thanks I'll do that."

The next morning, Angus phoned Charlotte.

"I'm not coming over today. I need to get Mr Perry's report written and visit Graham in hospital."

"All right," she said. He could hear Elvis barking in the background. "Elvis, be quiet, I'm on the phone. Sorry, no problem. See you tomorrow?"

"Probably." He pressed the call end button.

Those weren't the only reasons he wasn't going over. He felt put out that Charlotte was tracking him.

He was short with her on the phone, and regretted it as soon as he'd ended the call. She didn't ask about Graham and simply accepted his explanation. Good, he thought. After all, it wasn't as if they were married.

The thought of being married to Charlotte whizzed through his brain, and he allowed himself to dwell on it. She was both infuriating and lovely, and she was starting to get under his skin. Everything she put her mind to, she was brilliant at. But then there was the small matter of her being a millionaire – no, multimillionaire. The thought of all that cash was like a brick wall, blocking him from making a move. Everyone would think he was only interested in her money. Why did he care what other people thought? He never usually did. He wondered what she'd been like before she was rich. Probably exactly the same, just no Bentley and a smaller house.

Anyway, the relationship had to stay platonic, for both their sakes. She was still messed up from her divorce, and he didn't want to complicate matters. And he quite liked being single, though lots of his friends seemed to use that as an excuse to try to set him up with any single woman they came across. But he was a creature of habit and he liked his own space.

Once the report on Mr Perry was written and sent, Angus started to look at the next case. It seemed the insurance company had a never-ending supply of claims for him to look at. The next one was for a stolen classic car - a Jaguar Mark II, just like the one Inspector Morse had. Classic cars weren't normally taken for money, because they were so unusual and often easily traced. But if the owner was an enthusiast and had got into financial difficulties, then claiming on your mildly valuable car could be a good earner. I'll make sure Charlotte checks the photos, he thought. That could save a lot of time.

In the afternoon, he phoned the hospital to ask how Graham was doing. As it turned out, he was still in theatre. And Graham's leg had caused another problem: there was no way he'd be able to do the Grizzly now, and Angus had been relying on their joint training for motivation. He wondered if anyone else could train with him, but he didn't know anyone following a similar schedule. He'd have to come up with something, or face the fact that he'd have to train alone.

Having spent a day away, Angus was ready to face Charlotte again. The next day, she beamed at him when she opened the door, and took him straight to her office. She pointed at the far wall. "I've done a conspiracy board for Robert Hubbard's murder."

Sure enough, there was a board, covered with photographs, text, string and pins. It wasn't a bad idea – in fact it was a good focal point for the investigation – but it wasn't their investigation anymore.

He turned to face her. "Charlotte, why are you investigating a murder that your brother is looking into? It's not like we're getting paid for this."

"I know, but this is a lot more interesting than insurance fraud. Don't you think?" She had the brightness in her eyes which he'd seen plenty of times before when she was into something.

"I guess so. Look, I won't stop you doing anything you want to..." Her smile was still there. "But for the record, I think you should leave it to the police."

She studied the board, then looked at him. "Do you need me to help you with the insurance fraud?"

"I can always use some help."

"Okay, but can you at least have a quick look at the board, as payment for helping?"

He gave a curt nod and walked over to it. The board was very thorough, as usual. Charlotte had clearly been working hard to discover possible suspects for the murder.

The office door was nudged open and Elvis came in, tail wagging. When he saw Angus, he stopped dead, growled, then barked.

Angus sighed. "Still hate me?" He took a step towards the dog. Elvis barked again and started to shake.

"Come on now, Elvie, don't be a grumpy boy. Uncle Angus is nice." Charlotte picked the dog up and stroked his head.

Elvis licked her face.

"Eurgh!" Charlotte laughed. "I'll take him to my room."

Angus nodded, then turned to the conspiracy board again.

When Charlotte returned, he pointed to some names and photos. "Tell me why these people are on here."

"Oh, they're people who I know were associated with

him. Including his ex-girlfriend, who was plastered all over his Facebook page and his Instagram timeline a couple of years ago."

Angus's phone rang. The display said it was Woody. He answered it straight away. "Woody, how can I help you?"

"All right, mate," Woody replied. "Are you with Charlie?"

"I am."

"Put me on speakerphone. I've got something to tell you both."

Angus did as he asked and set the phone down on the desk.

"Well, hello, brother," said Charlotte. "Do you have news of the murder?"

"I do indeed. We've arrested our prime suspect."

Charlotte clapped to hands. "Oh, that's brilliant – you were quick! Who is it? Can you tell me?"

"I can, dear sister." He was silent for a moment. "It's your friend, Katrina."

Chapter Nine

"Katrina? You're not serious?" Charlotte's eyes widened.

"I'm deadly serious. We've arrested Katrina for the murder of Robert Hubbard."

"What on earth makes you think she did it? She wouldn't hurt a fly." Charlotte's voice was high pitched and panicked.

"Well, for a start, she was one of his victims..." He paused again, and they heard people talking in the background. "Yeah, she's admitted she knows he catfished her. We have mobile-phone evidence that pinpoints her exact location at Hubbard's house in Sidmouth during the time-frame when he was murdered. And there isn't any evidence pointing to anyone else who might have done it."

Charlotte sat down in the nearest chair. "You tracked her mobile to the nearest mast?"

"Yep, and it puts her right at the scene of the crime when it would have been committed."

Charlotte ran her hands through her hair, then looked at Angus. He appeared as stunned as she felt.

Angus shook his head. "Even if Katrina was there, it doesn't mean she did it. The murderer could well know that taking their mobile phone with them would mean they'd be tracked."

"You're right about that, but she's got a motive and no alibi. We'd be stupid beyond words not to arrest her," Woody stated.

Charlotte stood up and paced. "When did you arrest her? Have you questioned her?"

"Not yet, we're doing that later. We're just waiting for the duty solicitor."

"My friend is *not* going to have a duty solicitor. Wait, and I'll send my lawyer."

"I knew you'd want to get her good legal representation."

"Thanks, Mark. But you're still completely wrong about Katrina. She wouldn't hurt anybody."

"I hope you're right."

As soon as the call had ended, Charlotte called her lawyer and instructed him to go to the main Exeter police station to help Katrina.

Angus walked over to the conspiracy board, and noticed that Katrina wasn't on it. Of course she wouldn't be. No one would nominate their own friend as a possible suspect for a murder. Not unless you secretly didn't like that so-called friend.

"What is my brother like when he interviews suspects?"

Angus frowned. Should he tell her the truth? If it was a good cop, bad cop kind of interview, Woody was always the bad cop. He was unrelenting, so much so that Angus had often wondered whether he'd received military training.

Charlotte's eyes narrowed. "Why are you taking so long to answer that question?"

"If Katrina is innocent, Woody will find out. You have to trust him. He's a good policeman. He'll get to the truth."

Worry was etched on Charlotte's face. "There's only one way to make absolutely sure Katrina doesn't get charged with murder. We have to find the real murderer."

Angus nodded. He turned to the conspiracy board. "Go through these people, and tell me why they're on here."

Charlotte pointed to the first person on the top left. "This is Harry Reeve. He's a local pig farmer just outside Sidmouth: Colycombe Farm. It looks like he sells drugs on the side; in fact, I think he's got a cannabis farm there."

Next, she pointed to a photo of an attractive brunette, obviously a selfie. "This is Robert's ex-girlfriend, Abigail. She works in a beauty salon and nail bar. From what I can gather, they went out for four years. I haven't been able to find out why they broke up, but judging by the Facebook posts she made just afterwards, they didn't stay friends."

Her finger moved to the next photo. "This is Robert Hubbard's brother. They don't get on because of something to do with a family gathering where they had a bust-up."

At that moment, Elvis ran into the room, barking. He stood in front of Angus, yapping and growling, then backed away. Angus looked at the dog, then Charlotte, in a silent plea.

She went over to Elvis and picked him up. "There, there, Elvie baby. How did you get out? You're a little Houdini, escaping all the time. Uncle Angus won't hurt you. Will you?" Elvis wriggled excitedly in her arms.

Angus took a step away from them both.

Charlotte put Elvis outside the office door and closed it, then turned back to the board. "The last thing is a big gap." She indicated a large blank area which just said "Criminal Gangs". "He was clearly up to a number of bad things on the dark Web that would have involved gangs. So I've added a section for that; however, because he used TOR, I haven't been able to get anything from his computer."

Angus studied the board. "Chances are it was the gang. It usually is." He glanced at Charlotte. "Proving it might be difficult if we don't even know who they are."

Later in the afternoon, Woody rang Charlotte.

"All right, Charlie," he said in his usual happy tone.

"Mark, when are you going to release Katrina? That is why you're calling, isn't it?"

"Her lawyer has arrived; thank you for sending him. But we're keeping her in custody for another twenty-four hours."

"Why?"

"Why do you think? To question her further."

"You mean you're going to try and force her to admit she did it."

He sighed. "Look, I'll be in touch."

"I want to visit her," Charlotte demanded.

"You can't."

"That's so unfair. She's alone in a cell, and you're trying to pin a murder on her."

"She's going to be questioned again shortly. And you've got her an expensive lawyer. That's all you can do for now. Look, I've got to go. Come over for dinner tonight and I'll tell you more."

She'd wanted to tell him where to stick his dinner, but his hook had worked; she was desperate to find out more.

She ended the call and sighed.

Angus had been sat silently listening to Charlotte's side of the conversation.

"I take it they are keeping her in for longer?" he asked.

"Yes, but my lawyer has arrived and will sort it out. They're the best money can buy."

"I don't doubt it. Look, try not to worry. The truth will come out."

In the evening, Grigore drove her to Mark's house in the Bentley. He lived with his wife, Fiona, in a village just outside Exeter. As she got out, Charlotte noticed Angus's black VW Golf parked outside. Woody hadn't mentioned that Angus has been invited, too, but she was happy about it. He hadn't mentioned it when he'd left earlier, so maybe Woody had invited him after he'd asked her. Either way, having Angus there was comforting.

Her sister-in-law, Fiona, answered the door and they hugged. "Hello, darling, come through." Fiona was dressed in jeans and a blue shirt, her mostly silver hair in a shoulder-length bob. She'd been like an older sister to Charlotte for as long as she could remember. Fiona was in her mid-fifties now and had started dating her brother when she was nineteen and Charlotte was twelve. Their sisterly bond had grown over the years, and Fiona had been Charlotte's rock when her marriage had broken up.

In the lounge, Angus sat on the sofa, Woody in a chair. Both were each holding a bottle of beer, and stopped talking the moment she entered.

"Hello, Angus." She sat next to him on the sofa. "Mark," she snapped, not looking at him.

"That's not very nice, little sis. Still mad at me for arresting Katrina, then?"

"I'm not mad at you. I'm furious." She folded her arms.

"Come on now," said Woody. "As it happens, I don't think Katrina is the murderer. I think she was in the wrong place at the wrong time, but we haven't got much else to go on. So, for the time being, she's still our prime suspect."

"So you're still going to investigate her, because you can't find anyone else."

Mark rubbed his forehead. "We'll get to the bottom of it; don't you worry."

The doorbell rang and Woody stood up. "That'll be the takeaway," he said and left the room.

Angus gave her a brief smile. "Look, I know this feels awkward, but Woody will get to the bottom of this. He's really good at his job."

Charlotte knew he was right, but all she could think of was Katrina alone in a police cell. She gave him wry smile.

There was a kerfuffle in the hallway as Woody got the food from the delivery driver, and then they all went through to the kitchen-diner. Places were already set, and Fiona unpacked and set out the food.

"I hope you don't mind an Indian takeaway," Fiona said, unpacking the foil trays. "We couldn't face cooking this evening. I ordered your favourite, chicken tikka biryani." She looked over to Angus who was standing by the table. "And Mark said to order you a lamb jalfrezi. Is that okay? You can swap with me if you prefer a tikka masala?"

Angus shook his head. "Jalfrezi is perfect, thanks."

As they all sat and ate, Charlotte talked to Fiona about anything except Katrina. She kept one ear open to Woody and Angus's conversation, but most of it was about current police matters and old colleagues.

Eventually, when they had finished eating, Woody looked at Charlotte. "Hopefully you won't be so grumpy with me now that you've got some food in your stomach." He turned to Angus. "She's always suffered from being hangry: hungry-angry, have you noticed?" He laughed.

"Even as a little girl, she'd get really grumpy and crazy, a bit like a Tasmanian devil. Give her something to eat and she'd calm right down." He smirked at Charlotte. "You haven't changed a bit, have you, sweetheart?"

Charlotte gave him a contemptuous look. "If you're trying to get on my good side, you're failing dismally. Trying to embarrass me in front of Angus won't make my anger go away."

Woody took a swig of his beer. "You're really cross with me, aren't you? And after all the favours I've done for you. Remember what I did to your ex-husband and his new wife?"

Angus looked up from his plate and raised an eyebrow.

Charlotte shot Woody another harsh look. "Are you trying to put me off my food by mentioning Idris?"

Her brother grinned. "Have you heard from him lately?"

"Thankfully, no. And if you are trying to deflect the conversation away from Katrina, it's not working."

Fiona leaned in to change the subject. "Mark said you freaked out at the dead body."

Charlotte grimaced. "Yes. I'm not sure why."

"It was your first; it's always a shock. Although, you did well to get to your mid-forties before seeing one. I suppose it depends on your line of work." Fiona had worked as a nurse for twenty years. "You should try some visualisation. It's brilliant – works for me every time. There are all sorts of studies which say that if you visualise something, it fools your brain into thinking you actually did it. Athletes use it all the time, and they swear by it."

Charlotte wrinkled her nose. "Really? Are you sure it's not just a load of BS?"

"I've used it a few times, actually," Angus said.

They both looked over at him. "What did you visualise?" asked Charlotte.

Angus looked down at his plate, clearly weighing up whether or not to tell them. "You have to promise not to laugh. Or tell anyone."

"I swear," Charlotte said, her interest piqued.

He raised his eyebrows at Fiona and Woody, and they both nodded.

He sighed. "Flying. I hate it."

Charlotte's eyes widened. "Why flying?"

"Well, being in an enclosed space thirty thousand feet in the air. It freaks me out."

Charlotte leaned towards him. "And visualisation worked?"

He pushed up his glasses. "Pretty much." Then he looked at his watch. "I need to go soon. I've got to be up early tomorrow for a long run." He turned to Woody. "What was it that you wanted to update us on with Katrina?"

Woody shrugged. "Like I said earlier, I don't think she did it. It's just circumstantial evidence at the moment. I think the forensic evidence will come back that it was someone taller and stronger than her. She's petite."

Charlotte sat up straight. "I knew it!"

"Only because, despite the mobile phone evidence, there's nothing else that points to her doing it. She had a motive, but honestly, statistically, it's usually men who murder, not women. So rather than try and pin it on her, I'm looking for reasons to get her off the hook."

"So you think she was just in the wrong place, at the wrong time?"

Woody nodded. "I'm not into framing someone. My gut instinct is telling me she's innocent, and my gut's never been wrong yet. What do you think, Angus? Tell us, honestly. Ignore the fact Katrina is Charlie's friend." He picked up his beer and took a sip.

Angus pondered for a moment, his gaze going from Woody to Charlotte. Charlotte was looking at him with an expectant expression. "My gut is telling me she's innocent too."

Charlotte let out a sigh of relief. "Well, that's settled. We all just need to find out who did do it."

Angus stood up to go. "We'd be better leaving it to Woody and his team."

Charlotte was about to argue. She had no intention of leaving it to Mark but she simply smiled. "See you tomorrow."

Woody saw Angus out, then came back into the dining room and sat down. "So what's going on between you two?"

Charlotte met Woody's gaze. "Absolutely nothing."

He poured some more water into her glass. "But you'd like it to be something, wouldn't you? I saw the way you looked at him. Like a lioness about to pounce on her prey."

"Of course I do. I like working with him, but it's torture not being able to do anything about how I feel."

"What's stopping you?"

"He's not interested."

"What makes you think that?"

"I made a pass at him and he turned me down."

He gave a sort of snort. "You made a pass at him? When?"

"The first day we met."

"The first day! Bloody hell, Charlotte. You don't waste time, do you?"

"It was in the evening," she said defensively. "I'd had a

70

few drinks and he came over, and I kissed him, and he stopped me."

Fiona tutted at Charlotte's faux pas. Woody's shoulders shook as he tried to suppress a laugh. "Well, sis, you know Angus better now. Haven't you worked out that he isn't the sort of man to jump straight into bed with a woman he's just met?"

Charlotte's eyebrows shot up. "Some men don't do that?" She looked at Fiona for confirmation, who nodded. "Even if that's true, he hasn't shown any interest in me, not in that way. He's not given me even an inkling."

"But there could be many reasons why he hasn't made a move. For starters, your money."

"Really?"

"Yep."

Fiona leaned forward. "Darling, you were all over the place emotionally when you met him. You're doing brilliantly now, but maybe he doesn't want to ruin your recovery."

A glimmer of hope swelled in Charlotte. Then she groaned. "I have absolutely no idea what to say to him. It's like being a teenager again, fancying a boy but not knowing what to do. Mark, can you ask him whether he, um, feels something for me?"

Her brother held up his hands to ward her off. "Oh no, I am not getting involved in your love life. You're on your own there. You need to sort it out yourself."

Charlotte gave Fiona an expectant look, but Fiona shook her head with a smile. "I'm staying out of it too. But I have to say, good choice. He doesn't strike me as a cheater."

Charlotte sat back in her chair. "Should I kiss him again?"

"I don't think that's a good idea," said Fiona, barely

suppressing a laugh. "It might take him by surprise. You could just tell him how you feel."

"If I tell him and he's still not interested, he'll want to stop working with me, and I can't risk that. Working with him has done wonders for my mental health, even if some of it's boring. Insurance fraud and following errant spouses isn't exactly what I had in mind."

"That's the problem with detection: most of it is boring. Sorry to break it to you," Woody stated.

"But now I have to prove Katrina is innocent, so that will keep me busy."

He nodded at her. "You always were too clever for your own good."

Chapter Ten

The next day, Angus got up early to run. He needed to do 22K, so was on the road by six thirty. He'd finished by 9.00 am, but it wasn't the same training alone, and he was disappointed in his time. He lacked the same motivation he'd had training with Graham and was starting to wonder whether he wanted to run the Grizzly at all. By nine thirty, he was dressed and eating breakfast, still disconsolate. He was glad when his phone rang.

"There's been a development in the case," said Woody.

Angus shifted uneasily in his chair. Hopefully, for Charlotte's sake, they'd found a reason to let Katrina off the hook.

"The murder victim wasn't Robert Hubbard. It was his brother Andrew."

"What?" Angus put his toast down and pushed up his glasses.

"Yep. We all assumed it was Robert Hubbard, since the murder took place at his house, but a DNA test showed the body was that of Andrew Hubbard. He'd been arrested for assault a couple of years back and let off with a caution, so his DNA was still in the database."

"Okay, so where is Robert Hubbard? Is he your prime suspect now?"

"No. Robert is currently on his way back from Bangkok. He's been on holiday. His brother was house-sitting for him."

Angus let out a breath. "Was he coming back anyway, or is he coming back because you've told him?"

"He's on his way back anyway. He's mid-air right now, landing at Heathrow in a couple of hours. I've arranged for some Met officers to meet him when he comes out of customs."

"Have you told Charlotte?"

"Not yet. I've got tons on. Would you mind?"

"Yeah, sure."

Angus ended the call and immediately called Charlotte. It went to voicemail. *Hi, this is Charlotte. If you're listening to this message, it means I'm trying to avoid you. Don't expect me to call you back.*

He couldn't help smiling. He didn't bother leaving a message; she'd see the missed call and ring him back when she could.

Thirty seconds later, his phone rang. It was Charlotte. "Where are you?" he asked.

"At the farm-shop café. I wanted breakfast and didn't want to cook."

Angus had never seen Charlotte cook anything: not even toast or a sandwich. He wondered if that was because she couldn't cook, or she couldn't be bothered.

"I'll come and meet you. I have news of the case."

Fifteen minutes later, he sat down opposite her at a

table. The café was an extension to the main shop, with light-brown beams and white walls.

"I ordered you a coffee." She pushed a cup towards him. "What was so important that you couldn't tell me over the phone?"

"Thanks." He took a sip. "Your brother called me with an update on the case."

She raised her eyebrows. "Go on."

"The murder victim wasn't Robert Hubbard. It was his brother, Andrew."

"What!"

"I know." He took another sip.

"But..." She sat silent for a moment, processing the information. "But didn't you see it wasn't Robert when we found the body? You saw his social-media posts."

"I didn't; you just told me about them. And you didn't see the body."

Charlotte covered her mouth with her hand. "How did Mark work it out?"

"DNA test. But apparently, the two brothers look similar. Same height, hair colour and build. When we saw Hubbard that day, he had a baseball cap on which hid most of his face."

"What was Andrew doing at the house? Where's Robert?"

"Andrew was house-sitting. His brother's been in Bangkok, on holiday."

Charlotte shook her head. "So hold on ... was it still Robert behind the catfishing?"

"Andrew was only there temporarily, dog-sitting, so the catfisher probably was Robert."

Charlotte stared in front of her, her hand on her teacup.

"But I saw data going from that computer to the victims when Robert was out of the country."

"Maybe Andrew knew about it, and he was helping him with his scams as well as looking after the dog." Angus frowned, and glanced under the table. "Where is the dog?"

"I left him at home. He's started humping anything and everything, and I didn't want people to stare." She met Angus's eyes. "Do you think the murderer got the wrong person?"

"It's likely. If it was Katrina, then she didn't kill the man behind the scam, but his brother."

Charlotte pushed her cup away. "I really need to speak to Katrina. Are they going to charge her?"

"Woody didn't say, but they'll have to release her soon. They don't have any evidence apart from her mobile phone being in the area, so my guess is that she'll be out before the day is over."

Chapter Eleven

As it happened, Charlotte's lawyer phoned her a few hours later to tell her that Katrina had been released and was on her way home.

Charlotte and Angus set off straight away in the Bentley, driven by Grigore. Angus had got used to the car now, and also her driver, a short, heavily built young man with a pudgy face and dark hair. He was Helena's nephew, but Angus couldn't see a resemblance. He'd come over from Romania a few years ago, when Helena had been in an abusive relationship, and helped to sort out the ex.

At first Grigore had treated Angus with suspicion, which in hindsight was perhaps a good thing. Angus was growing increasingly fond of Charlotte, and having someone to watch out for her was a good idea. Being so rich meant that she was at higher risk of fraud, kidnap and goodness knows what else. His daughter Grace would call him old-fashioned for having such feelings, and Charlotte was an independent woman, but it never hurt to have some muscle around just in case. And Grigore fitted the bill very well. He was a man of few words, so although he didn't say much to Angus, the lack of a threatening demeanour meant that he liked him. Occasionally, Angus would even get a nod or a half-smile.

Inside, the Bentley was plush. The cream leather seats had lots of room, and were heated so that the cold weather was no problem. Next time he bought a car, he'd make sure it had a heated driver's seat.

"How far is Katrina's house?" he asked, as soon as they'd set off.

"Not far; she's on the outskirts of Tiverton."

Angus nodded. Tiverton was a small town fifteen miles north of Exeter.

When they pulled up, Charlotte unbuckled her seat belt and turned to face Angus, looking concerned.

His brow furrowed. "What is it?"

"Katrina can be a bit ... emotional at times. I suspect this will have pushed her over the edge. If she's a blubbering mess, that's probably a good outcome."

Angus undid his own seat belt. "I've dealt with hundreds of victims over the years. I'm sure I can deal with another."

"I didn't mean it like that. It's just that she's my friend, and it's different when it's someone you know well."

Angus got out of the car, and Charlotte followed.

Katrina's house was an end terrace on a new estate near the motorway, and it looked no more than a few years old. Like most of the new estates they were building all round Exeter, the houses were oppressively close together. Angus was thankful that while his own house wasn't huge, it wasn't crammed in like these.

Charlotte knocked on the door. There was no answer. She knocked harder, then bent and shouted through the letter box. "Trina darling, answer the door. I know you're upset, but we're here to help."

The flap snapped shut with Charlotte's fingers inside. "Ow!" She worked her fingers free, then shook her hand and knocked again.

An elderly man stopped with a black cockapoo. "She's not been out of the house since she got back." The dog sniffed around their feet.

"Are you a friend of hers?" Angus asked.

"Wouldn't say that, but I live down that end and we've met on the residents' committee. She don't say much."

There was a click behind them and the door swung open. All three of them turned to see Katrina standing in the doorway.

Chapter Twelve

A ngus felt a pang of sympathy. When he'd first met her, a few days ago, she'd been smartly dressed, with carefully styled hair and wearing makeup. Now she was wearing tracksuit bottoms and a plain white T-shirt. Her hair was pulled into a rough bun, and judging by the dark patches under her eyes, she hadn't slept for days. That wasn't surprising, seeing as she'd been in a police cell.

"Oh my goodness, Katrina, look at you!" Charlotte cried. She stepped forward and hugged her. The neighbour made a hasty retreat, leaving Angus on the doorstep.

Katrina started to sob into Charlotte's shoulder. After a moment or two, Charlotte gently prised her away and looked into her wet eyes. "Don't worry, my love, we're here to help. Everything is going to be all right."

She led Katrina into the lounge and made her sit down on the settee, then took hold of her hand. "Angus and I will do everything we can to find out who did this."

Katrina glanced at them both, her eyes red from crying.

Angus was reminded of the countless times he'd sat

with victims, then remembered the restorative power of a cup of tea. "Do you mind if I make us all a cup of tea? Then we can go over everything."

Katrina hiccupped. "That's thoughtful of you. The kitchen is through there." She pointed with a trembling finger.

As he made the tea, he heard Charlotte directing Katrina to breathe deeply to help her calm down. It seemed to work, and he wondered if that was one of the things that Charlotte's therapist Misty had taught her.

Five minutes later, they were all sitting down with tea. Angus took out his notebook and pen. "Let's start from the beginning. I'm going to ask you some questions. I'm not accusing you, just trying to work out how I can help, okay?"

Katrina nodded.

"I need to know everything you did after you left Charlotte's house, on the day she told you who the catfisher was."

Katrina sat back, her mug cradled in her hands. "I came home for a few hours, but I kept stewing over it. In the end, I decided I had to confront him. So I drove to his house. I sat in the car for at least half an hour before I drummed up the courage to knock on the door."

"Can you remember what time it was?"

Katrina shrugged. "About eleven thirty. But I can't be sure."

"What happened next?"

"I knocked and he answered quickly. I can't remember what I said; by the time I'd worked up the courage to confront him, I was furious at what he'd done. I barged into his house and just started shouting at him. We ended up in the lounge and I was screaming at him. I can't even remember what I said, but there was a lot of swearing."

Katrina wiped away a tear with the palm of her hand and sniffed.

"Did you threaten him?"

"No! I just wanted my money back. When I let him get a word in, he said he didn't know who I was and told me to get out." She turned to Charlotte. "I didn't believe him. I knew you wouldn't get it wrong, and I thought he was denying it because he was guilty. But it wasn't him, was it? It was his brother." She put her head in her hands and took a deep breath.

"Then what happened?"

"I stormed around the house looking for his computer. When I found it, it was switched off. I shouted at him that it would have all the evidence on it, so I pulled the wires out and tried to take it, but he grabbed me. Then he picked me up around the waist and threw me out of the house."

She started to sob, and Charlotte put an arm around her. Angus made notes of what Katrina had said and waited for her to stop crying. It took several minutes.

"Did you go back in the house?" he asked.

"No. I banged on the door but he didn't answer, so I went back to my car, and after a few minutes I drove away. I thought he might have called the police, but he didn't."

"Did you go back later?"

"No, I didn't.' She lifted her chin. "He was alive when I left. Yesterday, when the police arrived, I thought that either they'd done something about his catfishing, or he'd reported me trying to take his computer. When they arrested me on suspicion of murder I couldn't believe it. I didn't ... I *couldn't* do something like that."

Charlotte took her hand. "We know, darling, we know."

Angus looked at Katrina, then Charlotte. She was sure her friend couldn't murder someone. For now, that would have to be good enough. Investigating this would certainly be interesting and different from the usual cases. Last night he'd told Charlotte he didn't think Katrina was guilty, and he still believed it, but he always kept an open mind until all the evidence had been uncovered.

"Is there anything else you can tell us about this?" he asked. "Did you tell anyone about the situation, or that you'd gone to see him?"

"No one," she said firmly.

Angus scanned her face; there was something she wasn't telling them. He couldn't describe the sixth sense he had when he knew someone was holding something back – but it was definitely there.

He raised an eyebrow and Katrina's demeanour changed. She hesitated, shifted in her seat, then said, in an uneasy tone, "Well, I might have told some other people about him."

Charlotte let go of her hand. "What do you mean? Who?"

"It was on Facebook."

"Facebook?" Her eyes narrowed. "I don't remember you posting anything."

"It wasn't on my timeline; it was in a group."

Charlotte sighed and put her hand over her eyes.

"What group?" Angus asked.

"It's called Catfish Victims Devon."

"What did you post?"

"Just that I'd got hold of the person behind my scam and that he lived in Sidmouth."

Angus took a deep breath. "How many people are in this group?"

She paused a moment, thinking. "I'm not sure. Maybe three hundred."

Charlotte whipped her phone out and opened Facebook. In a few moments, she'd found the group. "There are three hundred and nine members at the moment. I'll join the group. At least it's private and not public, otherwise I'm not sure what we'd do."

"Do you think someone in the group killed him?" Katrina asked.

"It's possible. Did you tell the police you did this?"

"Of course I did. Your brother is horrible, Charlotte. He didn't believe a word I said."

Charlotte stared at Katrina. On the one hand, she loved her brother, on the other, she could well believe he was horrible to face in a police interview.

"I didn't put the whole address in the post, but the Facebook group administrator messaged me directly and asked for the full address. I was unsure about that, but he said that he keeps a list of known catfishers and sends information to the police. And he said there were vigilante groups who try to snare catfishers by pretending to be teenagers or children."

Angus nodded. The intentions of those groups were honourable, but they used entrapment. That wasn't viewed kindly in the courts, and many cases were thrown out before they got anywhere. "Did you tell anyone else the catfisher's full name and address?"

"Yes. One other person. She messaged me because she believed she'd been victimised by the same person."

"How did she figure that out?"

"They'd used a similar profile. You know, the stolen ID."

Angus tapped his pen on the notepad. "We'll need their Facebook profile so that we can talk to them."

Katrina nodded and drained her mug. "I'm so sorry for

all the trouble this has caused. If only I hadn't fallen for the scam in the first place. Then none of us would be sitting here."

"It's not your fault, Katrina; they scammed you," said Charlotte.

"What happens if they charge me, though? I mean, there's my mobile-phone evidence."

Angus shook his head. "That's circumstantial, and not enough to convict you at this stage; I'm sure of it. The phone evidence puts you at the scene at around the time the murder happened, but they'll need other evidence to secure a conviction."

Katrina brightened a little.

Angus and Charlotte left shortly afterwards, but not before Katrina had promised to phone Charlotte every day so that she knew she was okay.

In the back of the Bentley, Angus was quiet, looking out of the window. "Penny for them?" Charlotte asked.

He turned to look at her, smiled and pushed his glasses up his nose. "I'm not sure you'd like them."

"What do you mean?"

"Maybe you shouldn't be so ready to think your friend is innocent. I know she's your friend and you've known her for years, but that doesn't mean she wouldn't kill someone."

"But I know her."

"Remember the ABC of investigation, Charlotte. Assume nothing. Believe nobody. Check everything."

"Check everything," she chorused with him at the same time. "Yes, I know. I haven't forgotten what you've taught me. But you've changed your tune since our discussion with Mark."

"I haven't changed what I think. I'm just checking everything."

After a long pause, Charlotte asked, "Am I too soft?"

Angus studied her, then shook his head. "No. Don't change, Charlotte. It isn't soft to want the best for people, or to hope they're innocent. But I'm keeping an open mind because you have to, if you want to get to the truth."

"I want to get to the truth, too, you know."

"Even if that means she's guilty?"

Charlotte nodded. "We'll just have to agree to disagree for now."

"It's nothing to disagree about; it's just a simple matter of making sure we investigate everything."

"Did you really mean it when you said the mobile-phone evidence wasn't enough to charge Katrina?"

"Yes. If they don't uncover other evidence, it will be really difficult to get a conviction. However, the fact that she admitted to going in and trying to take his computer might work against her."

"But the fact that it's his brother means there's no motive for her to kill him."

Angus shook his head. "She thought Andrew was Robert at the time. But she's a small woman, and he was stabbed deeply. Physically, she *might* be able to do that. There's a lot of uncertainty." He glanced out of the window. "Anyway, when you've got the details of the Facebook administrator and the other person who knows the catfisher's identity, we need to talk to them straight away."

Chapter Thirteen

As soon as Charlotte got home, she started looking into the Facebook profiles of the two people Katrina had given Robert Hubbard's name and address to.

Angus made himself useful by preparing lunch. That was becoming a habit even in her home. He was a good cook, and although it was fairly simple food, Charlotte liked it, and also the fact that he made it for her. He always made well-balanced, simple lunches: none of the pretentious or strange foods some of her friends ate.

She sat at the breakfast bar with her laptop, looking into the profiles and surreptitiously watching Angus cook.

She jumped when her phone rang. "Charlotte," said Helena.

Charlotte smiled. "Hello, my love, how are you?"

"I have very bad news," said Helena. "You no like it."

Charlotte's heart sank. She wondered if it was about her two sons, or whether her investment banker had lost money. Yet lately, her investments had been doing remarkably well.

As for her sons, they were deep in study at university, and they'd both messaged a couple of days ago. She frowned. "Just break it to me, Helena. I'd rather know."

"You need have look at email I send you. It your bastard ex. He new Viper in *Vipers' Nest*."

Vipers' Nest was a hugely popular TV programme where multimillionaire entrepreneurs were pitched by business startups. They invested their own money, and a string of successful companies had been born out of it.

"*Vipers' Nest*? I love that show!" Charlotte opened her email, and found Helena's message. She clicked the link, which opened an advert on Facebook, and pressed play.

The video started with the *Vipers' Nest* logo and a large question mark. Then a voice-over said, "Who is the new Viper?" Then an image of Idris, her ex-husband, appeared. He was smartly dressed in a dark suit, a bright light behind him making him look angelic. The camera panned and he smiled directly into the lens. He folded his arms with a smirk and the voice-over continued. "Idris Beavin, multimillionaire tech entrepreneur, takes over as the new Viper. Will he be impressed by any of the startups bidding for his money?"

The scene changed to a close-up of him talking to a startup bidder. "You know, you remind me of my ex-wife. She always thought she was right too." He laughed.

The video finished with a shot of Idris sitting in the Viper's chair, with a huge pile of cash beside him. "The new series starts next week: Tuesdays, Channel Two, eight pm."

Charlotte was speechless."You okay?" said Helena, eventually. "Why they take on such bastard I not know."

"I didn't think I could hate him any more than I already did," Charlotte managed to say.

"I knew you no like it. You need time process. Remember, I'm here if you need me."

"I'll call you back."

Angus walked around the breakfast bar and looked at the laptop screen just as the video started again. Charlotte didn't want to see it again, but she thought she might be in a horrible dream. Sure enough, it was her ex-husband, Idris. And he had the nerve to criticise her on TV.

When the video finished, Angus looked at her. "Are you okay?"

Charlotte, still speechless, stared at him. When the video started for a third time, she slammed down the lid of the laptop. "If I hadn't stopped drinking, I'd down a couple of shots right now."

"It must be quite a surprise, seeing your ex on TV."

"To put it mildly. The cheek of him, calling himself an entrepreneur! I was the one who started the business; it was my idea. He just helped. I was the entrepreneur, I was the one who drove everything forward, and he just rode on my coattails."

"The best thing to do is not watch it. I found wishing my ex-wife, Rhona, the best was the only way of dealing with the issues we had."

Of course he was right; he was always right. But Charlotte fumed within. Idris had managed to humiliate her again, even though she hadn't seen him for over a year. Here he was, acting like he knew what he was doing. Like *he* knew how to build up a business. Well, if he did take on any of those poor entrepreneurs, they'd soon find out what a mistake they'd made. Not only that but he'd made a joke about her always thinking she was right.

Angus went back to the food and handed her a toasted panini, and when she bit into it, it tasted divine.

"Of course you're right, Angus," said Charlotte. "What he does now that we're divorced shouldn't affect me in any way. But he's still a lying cheat, and I'm not having that ad running everywhere." She picked up her phone.

"That's a good idea, Charlotte, call your therapist," said Angus. "Take your lunch with you."

She picked up her plate. "I'll call Misty right after I call my lawyers. Channel Two are going to wish they'd never run that ad."

An hour later, Charlotte emerged from her room to find Angus reading some papers. He looked up as she entered. "Did that help?"

"Yes, Misty always helps. And the lawyers are on the case. I'd nearly finished with the Facebook profiles when Helena rang. Give me an hour, and I'll have everything we need."

When Charlotte had the profiles ready, she turned her laptop round. "This is David Shaw, the administrator of the Catfish Victims Devon Facebook group. He set the group up himself just over a year ago. He lives in Ottery St Mary, which as you know is a town between Sidmouth and Exeter. He's thirty-eight years old, married to Sally, with one child aged eight. He works at a local supermarket."

"Do we know why he started the group?" asked Angus.

"No, we'll have to assume he was a victim. We can find out when we talk to him. He doesn't admin any other Facebook groups, and on his profile he generally only posts about boozy nights down the pub or visiting different motoring clubs. He's not on Twitter, but he is on Instagram, where he doesn't post much either."

Charlotte pressed a key and the screen showed a selfie of a woman sitting in a car. She had blonde hair and bright-red lipstick, and was wearing pale-blue work scrubs. "This is Jessica Abbott, a forty-eight-year-old care worker in Exeter. She doesn't post much on Facebook, usually photos of flowers or scenery. No other social-media profiles that I can find. She works in a care home in the centre of Exeter."

Angus got up. "Let's try the admin guy first."

Chapter Fourteen

This time Angus drove them to Ottery St Mary. It only took them half an hour and they entered the supermarket to find it fairly quiet. Angus went to the customer service desk and asked for David while Charlotte bought a bottle of water.

They heard the tannoy call for his name and he appeared about a minute later. Charlotte joined Angus just as he was introducing himself.

"How can I help?" asked David. He was dressed in his supermarket uniform, with a large white apron over the top.

"This isn't about work. It's about the Facebook group you administer. Is there somewhere we can talk?"

David led them to a quiet area by the handheld scanners. "I can't talk long; the management are always watching to see if anyone's skiving off. What's this about? Is it that bird Katrina? She's gone and got herself arrested, hasn't she?"

Angus nodded. "We're private investigators looking into the catfisher." He took out his notebook. "I understand she gave you the catfisher's name and address."

"Yeah, she did. I have a list of scammers, and I was going to report it to the police." He lifted his chin. "If she didn't, anyway."

"Do you do that a lot?"

"Sometimes. It's not often we actually find out who these people are, though. Most of them are in Russia or North Korea, or places like that. Certainly not in the UK. Well, not normally. I set the group up as support."

"Had you been catfished?"

He shook his head. "Not me, a family member: my dad. It affected him badly, so I have firsthand experience of it. I want to make sure we can stop as many catfishers as possible, and offer support to anyone who has been a victim."

"Did you visit him in Sidmouth?" Charlotte asked suddenly.

David turned to look at her. "No, I didn't. I just added it to my list, and I was putting a report together for the police. I reckon he got what he deserved, though."

"Well, it wasn't Robert who got murdered, it was his brother Andrew, who was house-sitting. Robert was out of the country."

"What?" David took a step back, staring. "Are you sure?"

"Yes, the police announced it late last night. It seems it was a case of mistaken identity. They did look similar, but it appears that the murder victim was in the wrong place at the wrong time."

David let out a long breath. "That's terrible."

Angus looked at his list of questions. "Have you met Jessica Abbott?"

David pursed his lips. "The name doesn't ring a bell. Where am I supposed to know her from? Give us a clue."

"She's a member of your Facebook group."

He smiled. "It's got over three hundred people now, so it's unlikely I'd remember one." He gave a small laugh. "Obviously a few people post a lot, but most just read the content. Everyone is too ashamed of what happened to them to talk much about it."

"And you didn't visit Robert's house at all, even though you knew his address?"

"I said that, didn't I?" he snapped.

"All right, thanks for your help." Angus closed his notebook and put it in his suit pocket.

"No problem. I hope you get the person who killed him, because that Katrina seemed nice."

Charlotte and Angus headed to the exit, but as Charlotte passed the magazine and newspaper stand, something – or rather someone – caught her eye.

Idris, on the front of a magazine.

It was *Your TV Choice*, one of those magazines with listings, gossip, and interviews with actors and presenters. "Hold on a minute, I just want to have a look at something."

She picked up a copy of the magazine. She felt as if she were dreaming, or possibly in the middle of a nightmare: "Meet Idris Beavan, the new Viper in the Vipers' Nest. He gives us all the gossip in this exclusive interview."

Charlotte seethed. She'd have to buy the magazine now, to see, and Misty would be furious with her. Angus probably wouldn't be happy either. But why should that matter to her?

When she got outside, Angus was waiting outside the car. "Got what you needed?"

"Not exactly. Just a magazine with my ex-husband on the front." She held it up.

"Are you sure Misty would approve?"

"I've already thought of that. And you're right, she'll tell me off. But I need to read this."

"Need to read it? Are you sure? It'll only set you back."

She frowned at him. "You make me sound like an alcoholic."

"Not in that way. It's just that you seem to have moved on, but when anyone mentions him, you fall to pieces. Why don't you give that to me, then phone Misty on the way back?"

Angus held his hand out. Charlotte hesitated, and was about to give him the magazine when a car passed them and broke the moment. "No, I need to read it." She hugged it to her.

He shrugged and got in the car.

Charlotte read the article as Angus drove back to Exeter. It wasn't even a proper interview, just a Q&A. The lazy type of journalism.

What made you want to join Vipers' Nest?

Well, I'm not a nasty person – ha ha! – but I've loved the programme for years. I've always wanted to be a Viper so that I can help entrepreneurs in the situation I was once in. You know, starting out without any support. Especially when you know you have a fantastic idea and you just need someone to give you a break.

"*What?*" she said out loud. She'd been the one to set up the company – it had been her idea! He'd been reluctant and it had taken her ages to win him round. It was only after she started to make some decent money that he came on board, quit his day job, and helped her build up the company. The whole time, she had been the one driving it forward.

What sort of entrepreneurs will you be interested in?
Any, really. Obviously my field is technology, but I just want to invest in a good idea and a passionate entrepreneur.

God help the entrepreneurs he helps, Charlotte thought. You're supposed to help, not just invest.

Are you worried that you're going to lose a lot of money?
No, not at all: I'm loaded! Ha ha. No, seriously, I'm in this to help others, but I'm only going to pick projects where I think I'll see a return. After all, I'm not a charity.

Charlotte pursed her lips. That's about right, she thought. Idris was never keen on giving money to charity. Whenever Charlotte did it, he told her off.

Now you're a successful and financially secure businessman, what motivates you to get up in the morning?
I love helping other people now that I've made it. I just want to pay it forward, if you know what I mean? I created a successful tech company from nothing, and I know what perseverance is. I can help people achieve what I did. And make more money from it!

· · ·

"The lying bastard. He didn't start the company. I did!" Charlotte muttered. She closed the magazine and threw it on the floor. "He's a lying, cheating, stupid, horrible man. I hate him."

"I take it the interview was good, then?" Angus said, with a slight smile.

Charlotte stared out of the window. Did she look like a crazy ex-wife? She didn't want Angus to think any worse of her. "He's putting on a persona which is a complete lie. It's all a front."

"I take it the interview doesn't mention him cheating on you with your best friend."

"Of course not. Now, that would be an interesting thing for the newspapers to find out, wouldn't it? That the new Viper is a cheating, lying scumbag. Yes, I think *The Daily Mail, The Express* and the *Mirror* ought to know, at least. That would be right up their street."

Angus glanced at her, but said nothing.

Back home, when Charlotte entered, Elvis ran up to her, wagging his tail and eager to be picked up.

"Hello there, boy." She scooped him up and he licked her face. She went into her office to check her voicemail, and there was a message from her lawyers about the TV advert with Idris. They'd piled the pressure on but hadn't had a definitive reply yet.

Charlotte sighed. The irony was that if the advert was out there on the internet it was out there forever. She needed to talk to Misty.

"I couldn't help myself," she explained to Misty on the phone later. "How could I NOT read an interview he'd given?"

"Charlotte, how many times do I have to tell you: ignore

him. Stop thinking about him and get on with your life."
Misty sounded exasperated.

"I know, I know, but he's going be on one of the most
popular TV shows. It's hard to ignore. I loved that show, but
I can't watch it now he's on it."

"Darling, if you are going to move on, you have to view
everything he does as background noise you have to ignore."

"That's easy for you to say. His face seems to be plastered everywhere at the moment."

"Even if it is, it will pass. Then the newspapers and
magazines will move on to the next TV show or person.
Look, on no account should you talk to journalists about his
affair. It will just drag you into it; you need to keep a low
profile. Being in the public spotlight is not good for anyone's
mental health."

Charlotte sighed. "I know."

"Promise me you won't do anything, and just ignore
him."

There was a long pause. "I promise," she mumbled. She
wasn't sure she was, though.

He was going to get lauded for being a successful
entrepreneur when half the work, if not more, plus the orig-
inal idea for the company, was hers.

It was all going horribly wrong, and yet again, the heart
of all her problems and stresses was her ex-husband. The
only thing that made her feel slightly better was Elvis, who
greeted her with excitement.

She considered going out and getting completely drunk.
That wouldn't solve anything, though, so she got Grigore to
drive her over to Angus's house instead.

"How did Misty react when you told her?" Angus
asked. He sat back down in his dining room, the table
covered in papers.

Charlotte glanced at them and frowned, ignoring his question. "You're working on another insurance case, not the murder."

"Only until you'd calmed down from the article. We need to visit Jessica."

Charlotte sighed. "Shall we go now?"

"Why not." He got up. "By the way, Woody phoned. They've spoken to Robert Hubbard about his brother. They haven't charged him with anything, but they're looking into his catfishing. He can't go home for the moment because it's still a crime scene, so he's gone to stay with a friend, the farmer. We need to go and speak to him and Jessica, ASAP."

Chapter Fifteen

The care home where Jessica Abbott worked was in the heart of the city, a short walk from the cathedral. Charlotte and Angus decided to visit her at work, so that the element of surprise would be in their favour.

The building was Victorian, and large enough to house at least twenty residents. They were let into the care home straight away when they asked to see her, and shown into a small waiting room near the main entrance. It had a few chairs and a small coffee table, with several copies of the care home's brochure. Charlotte picked one up and leafed through it. Neither of them sat down.

"Why do care homes always smell of insulin or disinfectant?" Charlotte commented as she scanned the brochure. "I bet they don't mention that in here."

"Is this what insulin smells like?" Angus asked.

Charlotte sniffed the air. "Yep. One of my friends is a Type One diabetic; insulin has a very distinctive smell."

"Aren't you going to hack their Wi-Fi?" Angus asked.

Charlotte shook her head. "I don't think it would be worthwhile. I mean, a care worker wouldn't have much time to use computers. When she posted on the catfish victim group, it was sporadic. That indicates it was from home."

A few minutes later, Jessica came into the waiting room. She looked like a slightly older, more frazzled version of her Facebook profile picture. She was late forties; her face had a sort of plain look that made her disappear into the background. But she stood out because she was over six feet tall and overweight. If she was on a rugby field, she wouldn't look out of place.

Angus introduced them both. "We're here because you're one of two people who had been told the address of a catfisher before he was murdered. Or rather, his brother was. Robert and Andrew Hubbard."

Jessica sat down in a chair and gestured for them to sit down, too, which they did. "Yes. I've spoken to the police. I have an alibi: I was here, working on the night shift." She folded her arms.

"Did you tell anyone else his address?" Angus asked.

"As I told the police, no." She stared at them both, waiting for the next question.

"Why did you message Katrina and ask for his address? She posted on the group that she had the details of a catfisher. Why did you want to know who it was?"

"I wanted to know whether or not it was the person who catfished me. She'd posted details of how he did it: the fake profile, and from the looks of it, they were the same person."

"And how were you catfished?"

"It happened about eighteen months ago, through a dating app. We started talking. He flattered me, and I fell for it. I'm sure I won't be the last either."

"How much money did they get off you?" Angus asked.

"Five thousand pounds."

That's not much, Charlotte thought. Then she remembered that it was quite a lot of money if you worked in a care home and weren't a multimillionaire.

"And did you ever find out who the scammer was?"

"No."

"Was there any reason for you to believe that the man Katrina found was the same catfisher who scammed you?"

"As I said, some of the photos used were of the same man, but apparently you can buy catfishing kits on the dark Web, so those photos are used by lots of people. I wanted to check it out, though."

Charlotte looked at Angus, eyebrows raised. Care workers weren't usually up on tech, and what went on on the dark Web. "How long have you been a member of the Facebook group?" she asked.

"I can't remember when I joined, exactly, but I like helping to hunt these people down. It makes me feel better about being scammed myself. If I had more time, I'd do more, but I've got to work here to pay off the money I borrowed. I don't have any savings, you see. I took out a loan when that catfisher scammed me. He said he needed money for a plane ticket to visit me."

"Where did he say he was from?"

"Tunisia." She sighed. "The first time I sent the money he said he didn't get it, so I sent it again, thinking something had gone wrong. Then he said he needed more, because the price of the plane had increased due to the delay. Then he said he needed money to pay for a carer to look after his elderly mother, and I sent that too. I can't believe I fell for it." She softened a little for the first time. "That was all a lie, though, to make me believe he was a caring man."

"I'm really sorry that you were ripped off," Charlotte said, and Jessica gave her a curt nod.

Angus broke the silence. "Did you do anything with the address?"

"Not much. I was surprised Katrina told me, to be honest. I just looked the address up on an internet map and looked at his Facebook profile. I had no evidence he was the one who scammed me, so that was it. And mine was definitely out of the UK."

"What makes you think that?"

"He'd post pictures of the town where he lived. It definitely wasn't the UK. It was too dry, for a start. I know a lot of catfishing accounts have stolen photographs, but he was definitely abroad."

"So why did you ask for the address, if Katrina said the scammer was in the UK and your scammer was in Tunisia?"

"Like I said, I help track down any catfisher."

Charlotte looked at Angus. She was starting to realise that the gut feeling Angus had talked about might actually be real. Jessica was clearly lying about something, but she couldn't put her finger on it.

Angus stood up. "I haven't got anything else to ask you."

"I haven't either," said Charlotte. "Thank you for your time."

Charlotte was the first to speak when they got in the car. "She's lying about something. Why would she want to know the name and address of a scammer and then do nothing with it? Her scammer was in Tunisia. I don't believe she was trying to help track him down. She was using that address for some reason."

Angus nodded. "I agree that she was lying about something; her body language was completely defensive. And she didn't hesitate to tell us that she'd been catfished.

That's unusual, because most people are really ashamed of it."

"Want me to try and hack her home Wi-Fi?"

Angus gave a small laugh. "I suppose you should."

"I'll do my best."

Chapter Sixteen

The following day, Charlotte was preparing to drive to Jessica's house when her phone rang.

"I've just had a phone call from your brother," said Angus.

"Do you two have your own phone line? He calls you all the time. Why doesn't he ever call me?"

"I have no idea. But he called me to say that Robert Hubbard has been murdered."

Forty-five minutes later, Charlotte and Angus were standing beside the River Exe, a few miles south of Exeter. There was a police cordon around part of the path and a footbridge. Several police officers and SOCOs were busy investigating.

On the way over, Angus had filled Charlotte in. The body of Robert Hubbard – the real Robert Hubbard, this time – had been found floating in the river by a dog walker, near a pub called The Swan.

"How do they know it's murder?" Charlotte asked.

"Apparently there was a head injury, of the kind only

someone else could have inflicted. They're not sure whether he died of that, or drowning. They'll know more after the post-mortem."

"Is the body in that tent?" Charlotte gestured towards a blue tent in the pub car park with "POLICE" written on the side.

"Yes, and your brother is dealing with it because he dealt with the other case." Angus shook his head. "Two brothers killed within days of each other. Someone really didn't like Robert Hubbard if they went after him this quickly."

"Their poor parents."

Angus nodded. "Will you have a look at the body?"

"No way. Is that why you brought me here, to help me overcome my fear of dead bodies? Well, that's one fear I'm willing to live with." She shook her head. "Hard pass."

"Come on, Charlotte. If you're going to continue as an investigator, the chances are that you'll see more dead bodies."

Charlotte's eyes widened. "Don't say that!"

"I thought you wanted to try and overcome your fears and move on with your life."

"Most of my problems stem from my ex-husband. It's just a completely rational fear. Only crazy people would look at a dead body out of choice."

"Why don't you just give it a go?"

"You're not going to give up, are you?"

"I won't force you to do anything; I wouldn't be that stupid. Let's do some visualisation to start with. Then your brain will have formed the neural pathways, and actually seeing the body won't be as traumatic."

"You should become a therapist," she said, deadpan.

He smiled. "Come and sit down on the bench, close your eyes and we'll do the visualisation. It works. I promise."

Charlotte was going to refuse, but the pleading look in his blue eyes and a feeling that he was right won her over. She suspected it would be hard to refuse him anything he really wanted.

She sat down and closed her eyes. "Just concentrate on the sound of my voice," he said. "Ignore the sounds from the crime scene."

His voice was low and mellow, and she loved the sound of it. Even if the visualisation didn't work, she'd certainly have a nice time listening to him.

"You're walking over to the blue tent. You stop outside the tent. I'm standing by your side." He paused for a moment. "I open the tent flap, and you step inside. I'm still with you." He paused again. This was working: so far she wasn't nervous. "The tent flap closes behind you. You are in the tent with me and Robert Hubbard. You look at the floor. A sheet is covering Robert. Someone pulls the sheet back, and you look at his face."

Charlotte's face contorted a little as she remembered the photos of Robert from his real Facebook profile. Smiling, standing next to his ex-girlfriend. She tried to imagine what Robert would look like after he'd drowned. "The sheet is put over the body again, and you leave the tent."

"Am I interrupting anything?" said Mark. After Angus's soothing voice, it was like a bucket of cold water.

Charlotte opened her eyes and a surge of disappointment went through her. She'd been enjoying listening to Angus's voice.

Angus stood up. "We'd just finished."

"Hello, brother," said Charlotte. "How goes the investigation?"

"All right. How are you doing?" He nodded to Angus, then went over to Charlotte and gave her a peck on the cheek. "Have you come to gawp at the dead bloke, then, if you're brave enough?"

"Something like that." Angus put his hands in his pockets.

"Can we have a look?" said Charlotte. "Angus has been trying to help me visualise seeing a dead body so that I don't freak out."

"Anything for you, dear sister. He's not in a bad way – well, he's dead." Woody laughed. "But he's not in such a mess that it'll give you nightmares."

"Any more idea on the cause of death?" Angus asked as they walked over to the tent.

"The doctor says it was probably drowning, but we'll see when they've done a post-mortem."

They stopped outside the tent and Angus turned to Charlotte. "Ready?"

Charlotte nodded, and took a deep breath. It was now or never.

Angus pulled the tent open and they stepped inside, just like he'd said in the visualisation. And sure enough, on the floor was Robert Hubbard. But there was no sheet over him. Charlotte gave a small gasp; she hadn't been ready to see the dead body straight away. She stared at it, then let out her breath. She gauged her feelings.

"It's not as bad as I thought. He looks like he's asleep." She paused a moment. "Is this long enough? Can I leave now?" Angus nodded, and she turned to go.

Outside the tent, Mark was talking to a uniformed officer. When he saw her, he came over. "Did that help, then?"

"It did. Angus is a wonder, isn't he?"

"He certainly is, sister, he certainly is."

They both looked at Angus, who was approaching them, and he pushed his glasses up his nose. "Have you got a main suspect yet?" he asked.

"Not yet. There's a distinct lack of evidence, which is suspicious in itself. The divers are coming shortly to look for the weapon. We've had uniforms scouring the riverbank, but they haven't found anything yet. I'll let you know if something interesting turns up."

Angus took out his notebook and pen. "What about an estimated time of death?"

"Between ten pm and one am last night, the doc says."

"Three hours? That's quite a long time." Angus made a note. "When you spoke to Robert Hubbard about his brother, did he give you a list of people who might want him dead?"

Woody shook his head. "He refused. Given the sort of people he was involved with, he wouldn't have been so stupid as to name them. In hindsight, it might have been a good idea."

"Well, I'm certain that Katrina will have a good alibi, seeing as she's innocent." They both turned to Charlotte.

"My sergeant is already on his way to see her," said Woody. "Don't you go warning her." He wagged a finger.

"I wouldn't do anything of the kind," said Charlotte, rather indignantly. "Anyway, she's innocent; she has nothing to hide."

"I thought he was in hiding at that farm," said Angus.

"We're trying to trace his last movements," Woody replied. "Obviously, his last movements were here."

"You think he was murdered here, then?"

"Yeah, there's blood on the bridge. It was definitely here."

Charlotte swung round to look at the bridge. "So you could check the mobile-phone cell-tower data to see who was here?"

"We could, but I'd put money on it being a burner phone."

Chapter Seventeen

On the way back to Charlotte's house, she didn't say much. But when Angus had parked on her drive, she turned to him. "Thanks for … you know, the visualisations. I wonder if there's anything else I can use it for."

Angus smiled. "Your ex, maybe?"

Charlotte pondered for a moment, then nodded. "I'll mention it to Misty next time I speak to her."

A few minutes later, they were looking at the conspiracy board in Charlotte's office. She'd moved the picture of Robert and added "deceased" underneath his name.

"I suppose we need to find out people's alibis," she said. "Although obviously my dear brother will be doing that too."

"We can certainly find out what Katrina was up to, in order to exonerate her," Angus replied.

"I'll call her in a bit, but she'll probably message me as soon as Mark's minion has gone."

Suzy Bussell

Angus continued to look at the conspiracy board. "It could be any of them. Or none of them."

"That's very vague."

"Sorry, but it's true. But I want to talk to that farmer, Harry Reeve. Robert was staying with him. If Robert went to him, they must have been close."

"Yes. We definitely need to find out what Jessica was lying about too."

"You go and get what you can from her computer. I'll talk to Robert's ex-girlfriend."

As usual, Charlotte got Grigore to drive her in the other car: a black BMW and parked down the road from Jessica's house. She'd found her address from a simple internet search on the electoral register. She identified Jessica's Wi-Fi easily and set her password cracker running.

Half an hour later, the program hadn't got the password. "Come on," she said out loud.

"It no work?" Grigore asked.

"No. Most people don't have a difficult password. Usually only people with something to hide have a complex one." Charlotte was even more convinced that Jessica was hiding something.

An hour later, she still hadn't cracked it.

"You vant go home?" Grigore asked. "You vant me stay vith laptop?"

"No, I'll give it another fifteen minutes. If it takes much longer, I'll have to think of something else."

When Angus had been in the police, he'd gone to some strange places to interview people, but hair salons and nail

112

bars were always some of the strangest. Why any woman would want to spend time and money on having her nails done never failed to amaze him. Having neat, tidy nails, even painted nails, was good, but the really long, pointed ones that seemed to be the fashion weren't particularly nice. Last week, he'd been in a shop and seen, or rather heard, the sales assistant's false nails tapping on the tablet computer screen. It was irritating. How she managed to do everyday tasks was beyond him. Charlotte didn't have ridiculously long, false nails. Hers were always neat and clean, which was perfect.

The nail bar was compact, with a row of tables, one for each nail technician. There were four in all, and each wore a mask to protect them from the chemicals they were using. There was a strong smell of nail varnish in the air, and of some other chemicals that made Angus's nose twitch. He wanted to get through this as quickly as possible.

Two nail technicians were male, the other two female, and behind the mask, the second along was Robert's ex-girl-friend, Abigail. If the technicians thought that a man coming in on his own was odd, none of them did more than give him slightly longer scrutiny.

Luckily, Angus only had to wait a couple of minutes before Abigail had finished with her customer. He approached her table.

"What were you after today?" she asked, looking at Angus's hands. "Extensions, or just a standard manicure?"

"I've not come for a service today, thank you," said Angus. "I'm Angus Darrow, and I'm helping investigate the murder of Andrew Hubbard." He shifted his weight from foot to foot and glanced at the others. "Is there somewhere we can talk in private?"

"I'm due a cigarette break; we can go outside." She

stood up and took her mask off, revealing her face. She had dark brown eyes that matched her straight, long dark brown hair that fell well below her shoulders. She was dressed in a salon uniform with the name of the nail bar embroidered on the front left "Abi's Nails".

There was a bench not far away from the shop. Abigail sat down, and Angus stood in front of her. She lit a cigarette and took a deep drag. "I heard his brother had been killed. Bit of a shock, that."

"I'm sorry to say that Robert has been murdered too."

Abigail's mouth fell open. "Robert's dead?"

"I'm afraid so. He was murdered last night; they found his body this morning."

"How? What? Where?" She stared up at him.

"He was found floating in the Exe, just near The Swan pub. The police don't have any more details at this time."

"I know that pub. My God, Robert and his brother killed, within days of each other. No doubt it was one of the dodgy dealers he spent so much time with." She sat forward, one hand on her knee. "I heard about Andrew, and I half-expected someone to come and talk to me, but I thought it would be the police. It hadn't been that long since we broke up. We were always breaking up and getting back together – it was like we both thrived on the drama – but this time it was a breakup for real, as far as I was concerned."

"Why was that?"

"He was seeing someone else behind my back. I could put up with his dodgy dealings, but not shagging another woman." She looked at Angus, then took another deep drag of the cigarette.

"When was the last time you saw Robert?"

She paused. "A couple of days after we broke up. He

came begging me to take him back, just like he always did. Saying he'd change and he'd never see what's-her-face again. Turned up here, actually." She jabbed her cigarette at the shop. "I wasn't happy; it disturbed the other customers."

"Did he get violent?"

"He got aggressive, but never violent." She shook her head. "I can't believe he's dead. And his brother got done in too. I mean, what sort of psycho kills a man and then kills the right one straight afterwards? That's just demented, isn't it?"

Angus stayed silent, sensing that her question was rhetorical. "Did you ever meet Andrew?"

"Oh yeah, loads of times. I didn't know him that well, though. They never got on, really, so whenever I met him, it was brief."

"Was Andrew involved with Robert's dealings?"

"No, not Andrew. He wasn't exactly straight, but he never got involved in Robert's stuff. That's why they argued. Andrew would just pass on a bit of weed when a friend wanted it, but Robert was getting large quantities of it and selling it to several dealers. I didn't like it either."

Angus scanned her face to gauge her reaction. "Did you know that Robert was scamming people online? Catfishing them?"

"No. That's what he was up to, was it?" She raised her eyebrows, then shook her head. "I guess I shouldn't be surprised. I knew he was doing something really dodgy online, but I thought it was just drugs. I never thought it was that."

"Did he contact you anymore after the day he came here?"

She pondered a moment. "A couple of times. A couple of phone calls I didn't answer, and a few texts too. After that, he stopped, and I wasn't sorry. I've been much happier since we broke up. You don't realise how toxic a relationship is until you're out of it."

Angus thought about Charlotte and her ex-husband, Idris. If she'd been here, she'd have sympathised with Abigail.

"Do you have any idea what happened to the dog, Elvis? He was one of the things we fought over. Most of the breakup was amicable, but this was the only thing we fought over. Elvis was my dog, you see, but he wouldn't give him back. In the end, I let him have Elvis because I thought it would stop him feeling alone and bothering me."

"Elvis is your dog?"

"Yeah, have you seen him? He's sweet; I really miss him. He used to sit with me in the salon every day, and he loved all the attention the clients gave him. Did the police take him to a dogs' home?"

Angus remembered how the little dog barked at him whenever he went near it. "Not exactly. He's with a foster carer at the moment; I'll speak to them."

"That would be amazing. I've missed him so much. Even though he humped my cushions." She laughed.

"Can you think of anyone who would want to kill Robert?"

She laughed, but her laugh had no humour in it. "It sounds like you've got a few people in mind. Once you find out who he worked with, that'll give you a few more. Otherwise, I don't have any idea. I'm sorry."

Angus closed his notebook and put it in his jacket pocket. "Thanks for your time."

She stood up and started to walk towards the nail bar, then paused and turned back. "Even though we split up, I didn't want him dead, you know."

Back at home, Angus prepared himself for an evening of training for the Grizzly. He was dreading it. It wasn't that he didn't like running, it was because he would have to do it alone. His friend Graham was still laid up with a broken leg, but he'd messaged him earlier to say that he was at least home now and being cared for by his dutiful wife. Angus made a mental note to visit in a few days with a get-well gift.

He'd been delaying the inevitable. He thought about putting a podcast on; he did that quite often when he ran. Somehow, though, the thought of having to run all that long distance on a trail filled him with dread. He thought about Charlotte and the visualisation they'd done. Maybe he should be doing that himself.

He'd just tied his laces when the doorbell rang. He glanced out of the window and saw the Bentley.

When he opened the door, Charlotte looked him up and down. "I know you're about to go on your run, but can I come with you? I've got an e-scooter in the boot. I could keep you company."

Angus smiled and nodded a yes. How had she known exactly what he needed?

"Thank you. If I stay in, all I'll do is watch my bastard ex-husband on TV tonight. This will distract me."

"It solves both our problems; I wasn't looking forward to running on my own. It'll take me a couple of hours, though. Are you sure you're up for it?"

"I am." She turned and nodded to Grigore, who got out, opened the boot and brought over an e-scooter and a helmet.

"It's a mixed-terrain scooter with big wheels. It's the best on the market," she said proudly. She put on her helmet. "Do you want me to ride beside or behind you?"

"If you knew the route I'd get you to go in front, but stick to the side for now."

It was getting dark when Angus finally got to the home straight. Charlotte was skilled at riding the scooter; he thought she must have had practice and wondered when that had been. She hadn't even been that distracting either. He'd assumed she'd talk all the time, but mostly she stayed quiet, only talking to him at the start and occasionally to ask about the route. That was unlike her. Perhaps she was thinking about her ex-husband, or simply enjoying the experience. At any rate, it had got her out into the fresh air. As far as he knew, Charlotte didn't have hobbies other than going to the spa or meeting friends for coffee.

Angus stopped his watch when they arrived back home. Two hours and forty-five minutes, which for twenty miles, was only a few minutes over what he'd hoped. He was still unsure whether the mixed terrain on his training runs had been mixed enough, but it would have to do, since the race was in a week's time.

He bent down, panting, and got his breath back. His legs longed for an ice bath to take the pain away.

A moment later, Grigore pulled up in the Bentley. Charlotte took off her helmet. "Well, that was certainly an experience. I think I had it easier on my scooter."

"Maybe you should take up running."

"I'd never be able to keep up with you. Or is that the point?"

He smiled at her assumption that they'd run together. "Thanks for keeping me company. It made all the difference just knowing you were there."

"You're very welcome. I'd better get back to Elvis and take him for some exercise."

"That reminds me; I haven't told you about my chat with Abigail, Robert's ex."

"Anything suspicious about her?"

"Not at all." Angus gave her the gist. "Elvis was her dog, and she let Robert keep him to placate him when they broke up. She'd like him back if possible."

"Elvis was her dog?"

He nodded. "I told her he was with a foster carer, but I didn't say who. Do you think you could give him up?"

Charlotte stood motionless for a moment. "I've got used to having a pet. I know he's a bit yappy and he doesn't like you, but I'm rather fond of him."

Angus pushed his glasses up his nose. "She said she even took him to work with her."

Charlotte sighed. "All right, all right, I get the idea. I'll give him back in the next few days."

Grigore picked up the scooter, walked to the car, and opened the back door for her. "See you tomorrow," said Charlotte, and got in.

Chapter Eighteen

The next day, Charlotte had a surprise visit from Katrina. "I thought you were ignoring me," Charlotte said, pouring her a cup of tea. They were sitting in her conservatory, the sun shining through the glass.

"Of course I wasn't ignoring you, darling; you've done so much for me. It was late when the police left, so I didn't want to bother you."

"What happened with the police?"

"They asked me what I was doing at the time when Robert was killed. I was home asleep, and my mobile-phone records prove it, so there's nothing they can do." She stirred her tea, then took a sip.

"Hopefully, now that it's a double murder, my dear brother will look for other suspects."

"I know: two people killed! That man's poor brother – what a shame. I can't say I'm upset about Robert, though. After all, he swindled money out of so many people. I don't suppose I'll ever see my twenty thousand pounds again."

"You know I can give you the money," said Charlotte.

"You're such a sweetie, darling. I might take you up on that offer."

"Good. I've made a packet on some recent investments."

"Well, one thing's for certain: I'll never make that mistake again. Anyway, where is that delicious man you work with?"

Someone's ears must have been burning, because at that moment the doorbell rang, and Helena showed Angus in shortly afterwards. Dressed as smartly as ever in a navy pinstripe suit, he looked a little tired from the run the day before.

Charlotte stood up. "Hello, Angus. Have you recovered from yesterday's run?"

"A bit achy, but otherwise I'm okay." He nodded to Katrina.

"Katrina popped in to let me know what happened yesterday."

Katrina uncrossed, then recrossed her legs as Angus approached, then fluttered her eyelashes. What is it with some women? thought Charlotte. Why do they behave so differently around men?

Katrina smiled at Angus. "I was just telling Charlotte that the police checked my mobile-phone data and discovered I was at home just like I said I was when Robert was murdered."

Angus nodded, and sat down.

Charlotte walked over to her new coffee machine and pressed the button for an Americano with milk. "My brother will just have to find the real murderer. At least this will shift any belief that you did it."

The coffee machine beeped and spluttered; it was out of milk.

"How far did you run yesterday, Angus?" Katrina asked,

as Charlotte went to the kitchen. When she came back, Katrina was in full-on flirting mode, running her hand through her hair and leaning suggestively towards Angus. Angus, meanwhile, was sitting very upright in his chair, answering Katrina's questions. That was just like him.

"Here you are." She handed him his coffee.

"Thanks. I suppose you two want to catch up. I've got a few things to work on, so if you don't mind, I'll go and work in the office."

"It's all right, I was going shopping anyway." Katrina stood up. "It's lovely to see you again, Angus. Thank you so much for all you're doing. I don't know what I'd do without you and Charlotte."

Charlotte saw Katrina out, and Angus went to the office. When she came back, she joined him. He was sipping his coffee and looking at the conspiracy board. At the side was a to-do list. It said "Farmer", then underneath, "Jessica – computer".

"I couldn't hack into Jessica's Wi-Fi," said Charlotte. "That's very unusual. But I've got a faster computer and a better program now, so I'll have another go ASAP."

"Maybe one time when we're investigating something, you could try not hacking into everyone's networks or computers." Angus pushed up his glasses and smiled.

"What a horrible suggestion. Anyway, hasn't it proved useful?"

"It has. I never know what you're doing, and it's better it stays that way."

"I'm not arrogant enough to think I'll never get caught, but I'm careful. Really careful." She walked to her desk and sat down. "You know, I really should get you a desk here."

"No," Angus said, a little too quickly. "I mean, it's your office. You don't want me hanging around."

"You're not in the way," she said, with a hopeful look.

Angus looked back to the conspiracy board.

"That's a no, then," Charlotte mumbled to herself. Best change the subject. "What do you think we should do first, hack Jessica or visit the farmer?"

"I vote the farmer," Angus replied.

She tapped a few buttons on the keyboard. "I was looking into him late last night. They open the farm up once a year for 'Open Farm Day', but the next one isn't for another six months, so that isn't an option. A web satellite search shows he's got lots of fields and barns, with outbuildings everywhere. It's basically the usual large Devon farm. He has dairy cows, but lots and lots of pigs. He even sells pork on his website, at a premium price, of course. Unusually, he also does some crops: onions mainly."

"Is that unusual?"

"Not really. And he has lots of job adverts for farmworkers on zero-hour contracts."

"Okay..."

"Instead of going and interviewing him, I thought I could go to the farm and pretend I wanted a job. Then I could have a look around and see what's going on."

Angus studied her. "I don't think that's a good idea."

"Why not?" asked Charlotte. "If he's shifting drugs, he won't admit it to us, will he? Robert Hubbard was selling drugs, and he had to get his supply from somewhere. He went to stay with him too. I definitely think the farmer needs a different approach."

"We wouldn't ask him directly about drugs," Angus replied. "It would all be around how he knew Robert, that type of thing."

Charlotte sat back in her chair. "He'll just lie. I can't see what harm it would do to have a nose around for a day. At least if I'm working there I can have a snoop. I can claim I got lost if they wonder what I'm doing."

"Are you just looking for excitement?" Angus asked. "Some kind of weird thrill from pretending to be someone you're not?"

Charlotte narrowed her eyes. "No."

"Farmwork is hard manual work. Are you up for that?"

"I'm no stranger to manual work," snapped Charlotte. "When I was a student, I had several jobs to pay my way. I worked as a cleaner in a local school during the week and every summer I cleaned factories. It was the filthiest, most disgusting work I've ever done. It was terrible pay too. Cleaning toilets and mopping floors made me work harder on my degree."

Angus looked rather sorry. "I apologise. I didn't know that."

"There's lots of things you don't know about me. It's only in the last few years that I've had lots of money. I appreciate every penny because I've worked for it, and I did plenty of crap jobs along the way."

The room fell silent and Charlotte turned back to her computer. A few moments later, Angus spoke quietly. "All right. I'll go and ask him some questions; you go and work there for a day, and we'll see what we can both find out. We're still working together, just taking on different roles. But why not get Helena to come with you, and make sure you have Grigore close by, just in case."

Charlotte looked up at him and smiled.

Chapter Nineteen

T he following day, at 6.oo am, Charlotte and Helena were walking up to the farm, dressed in old jeans and T-shirts. Charlotte had discovered that after Brexit, the number of farm labourers had decreased significantly. Grigore had dropped them off in the Volvo, far enough away for no one to see.

Ten minutes later they found themselves outside the farm office, a small rough building some distance away from the main farmhouse. The farmhouse itself was an imposing Victorian building which looked well-maintained. Charlotte mused that farmers always claimed they were poor, but this farmhouse didn't bear that out. Then again, the farm covered nearly two hundred acres, and if she was right, he had been supplementing his income illicitly.

Charlotte had briefed Helena beforehand. Helena had been happy to help, saying that some of her family and friends had come to the UK to work as farm labourers before Brexit, so she knew what to expect: long hours and not much pay.

A few workers were milling around, most of them men.

Judging by their weather-beaten state, they spent a lot of time working outdoors.

Helena approached a group of three loitering and smoking roll-ups. She said something in Romanian, and a couple of them smiled, replied and pointed to the office door.

"What did they say?" Charlotte asked when Helena returned.

"Register to vork through zat door vith farm manager."

Inside, the office was sparse and dirty. A man behind the desk gave them the once-over. He was in a tatty beige jumper and combat trousers. He yawned loudly and ran his hands through his hair which looked like it'd last been brushed a few years ago. "You've come to work for the day?" he said, in a West Country accent.

Helena stepped forward. "Yez," she said, in a thicker than usual Romanian accent.

"You here legally?"

"Yez."

The manager looked at Charlotte.

"She no speak English," said Helena. "I vill tell her vhat she needz do."

The manager harrumphed. "I'll put you two together, then. We've got a few tons of onions coming in from the field and they need the rough ones taken out. Starting in ten minutes and finish at six tonight. Half an hour for lunch and you can have three toilet breaks, but no more."

Charlotte tried to keep her face blank. What sort of working conditions were these? Three toilet breaks? She probably wouldn't need all three, but that was just nasty. And what about tea breaks?

Helena nodded and then spoke in Romanian to Charlotte. Charlotte nodded in what she hoped were the appropriate places. She'd picked up a few words of Romanian here and there, but she'd always struggled to learn foreign languages since she was a child.

Helena turned to the manager. "How much you pay?"

"Fifty pounds for the day. You get paid when you finish, cash in hand and no questions asked. If you do a good job, you'll get sixty pounds next time."

Charlotte stared at the wall opposite to force herself not to react. But if these were illegal workers and it was cash in hand... She made a mental note to find some reason to report these people to the police.

Fifteen minutes later, Charlotte and Helena were led with two other workers to a nearby barn. It had three sides, and was open to the main farmyard. Inside, an array of machinery lay dormant. There was a giant funnel where the crops were loaded and a conveyor belt which led to a packaging area.

The manager took them to the conveyor belt. "Check through the onions and pick out any bad ones," he said to Helena. "Tell your friend." Helena nodded and spoke to Charlotte again in Romanian, and Charlotte nodded.

It didn't take long for Charlotte to get into a rhythm. In a strange way, she quite liked it. She didn't have to think, just sort, and the sound of the machinery wasn't too loud.

The good thing about working in the barn was that she had a view of all the comings and goings in the main farmyard. The downside was that if she tried to hack the Wi-Fi, she'd be visible to anyone who passed by. She decided to wait an hour or so, claim she needed the toilet, and do it there. The other workers were too close for her to get out her mobile phone and start the process.

So about an hour and a half later, when she was starting to get really bored with sorting onions, Charlotte went over to Helena and told her what she was going to do.

The toilet, a chemical one, was just outside the sorting barn. How she hated those things. She'd regretted going to a few festivals because of the toilet facilities. There were never enough of them, you had to queue for ages, and once you got inside they were tiny, and you wanted to get out as quickly as possible. Maybe that was the point.

Charlotte opened the toilet door and a waft of urine hit her. Inside, it was as grim as she'd thought it would be. Worryingly, there didn't seem to be any soap, and when she pressed the foot pump for water in the sink, nothing came out. She took out her phone and started to hack the Wi-Fi. There was only one network, labelled "Colycombe" after the farm. She watched the screen as her program blinked at her. It took 6.78 seconds to crack the password: "sausage-sandwich". She shook her head in dismay at such an easily hackable password. All lower case, no numbers and no special characters made it super-easy to crack.

As soon as she was in, Charlotte planted her spy software to snoop on the network. It was untraceable, and would send information back to her while she was on the site. Once that was done, she left the toilet and took a deep breath of fresh air. She saw a car in the distance, coming down the lane towards the farm. A black VW Golf. Angus's car. She looked at her watch: eight o'clock. Typical, always an early starter.

She could have gone into the barn, but decided to wait a moment so that he could see her. About a minute later he pulled up, got out of the car and looked around. He saw her, and she smiled at him, but he didn't respond apart from a very slight nod. Then he went towards the farmhouse and knocked on the door, and Charlotte went back to the barn.

After another hour, Charlotte was thoroughly fed up with sorting onions. Angus had left half an hour ago so she needed to snoop around the farmyard, and the sooner the better. She had no intention of staying all day. There were lots of tractors and farm vehicles coming and going, but perhaps she could slip away during a quiet moment. The only thing she couldn't be sure of was whether the manager came to check on their work. If so, that could be tricky, but she'd have to risk it. She told Helena her plan, then slipped out of the barn twenty minutes later.

She started off with the nearest barn, which turned out to be the milking shed. Beyond were two large barns with open doors which showed they were used for hay storage. She walked behind them and saw some stables. They looked quite new, but there was no paddock. No one was about, so she went to them. There were three separate wooden stables, all securely locked, which seemed suspicious.

Charlotte looked away from the farmhouse and saw an old farmworker's cottage. It looked at least a hundred years old, and the windows were boarded up with black plywood. She went over to it. She tried the front door, and her heart skipped a beat as it opened. She pushed the door slightly open and listened for anyone inside. There was no sound, so she slipped inside, closing the door quietly behind her.

Inside, she felt a sudden wave of heat. A short hallway led to one room downstairs, and a bright light shone from it. She followed the light, and found herself in what felt like a tropical paradise. Rows of plants were everywhere, with daylight lamps shining down on them.

She took a closer look at the plants. The smell was strong; she'd recognised that as well as the leaf patterns. They were all the same kind: cannabis. "I *knew* you were up to something," she muttered. There must have been at least a hundred plants. That was what the farmer had been doing with Robert Hubbard. He was growing it, and Robert was selling it.

Charlotte took out her phone and snapped some photos, then videoed the plants. She would tell her brother later. Then she heard the outer door creak. "No!" she whispered.

Her eyes darted around the room, looking for the safest place to hide, and she saw a darker corner opposite the door. She hid herself just as footsteps entered the room.

"I think some of these need watering; they're looking limp," said a loud male voice. "They're thirsty, you know. We've got a water irrigation system going, but maybe we should turn it up."

"Look, that lamp's gone," said another voice. "Have you got any bulbs?"

"Yeah, in the stable. I'll go and get one. Come with me, if you want."

Two sets of footsteps receded, and Charlotte looked up. The faulty bulb was almost directly above her. If they came to change the bulb, they'd see her straight away. She headed out the main room, to the front door while they went to the stable. She peeked outside and watched them disappear inside.

A moment later she was outside. There was no point in staying any longer; she might as well go. She took out her phone and rang Grigore, who was stationed just five minutes away. "Don't come down the lane or it will look suspicious," she said.

Chapter Twenty

She went straight to the onion barn and nodded to Helena, who stopped what she was doing and walked outside with her. When they got clear of the farm buildings, they ran down the lane. Grigore was waiting just out of sight of the farm. They jumped into the car and he drove off.

In the car, she told Helena and Grigore what happened, and Helena wagged a finger at her. "You should no gone in building on your own."

"I know, but I couldn't help myself. I'll phone my brother when I get to Angus's house. Can you take me there? I want to show him too."

Grigore dropped her off at Angus's house and took Helena home.

"Did you find anything out?" Charlotte asked, as soon as he opened the door.

"Hello, Charlotte, do come in." He looked her up and down. "You've come straight from the farm?"

She nodded and slipped in.

He led the way to the kitchen. "You smell of onions."

She sniffed her T-shirt. "Sorry."

"No, I didn't find anything out. You were right; he didn't tell me anything at all. He denied he knew Robert Hubbard, or that he'd ever been to visit him. He's definitely up to something."

"Gut feeling?"

Angus gave a small laugh. "Yeah, something like that. You're back early."

Charlotte told him about the cannabis plants and showed him the photos and video.

Angus whistled. "You'd better get that over to your brother."

Charlotte nodded. "I will shortly. Despite the cannabis plants, I can't see why the farmer would want to kill Robert. I mean, if he was distributing the drugs, he would be shooting himself in the foot by getting rid of his distributor."

"I agree. The only possible motive he might have is if they'd fallen out for some reason, but Robert went straight to stay with him, so there's no evidence of that."

Charlotte sighed. "Well, at least we can cross him off the suspect list." She picked up her phone and dialled Woody.

When she put the phone down five minutes later, she suddenly realised she was starving. Angus made them sandwiches for lunch and then drove her home. She was eager to shower, to get the smell of onion off her hands and out of her hair and change her smelly clothes. By now, her brother and a team of police would be on their way to raid the farmyard.

As soon as Charlotte entered the house, Elvis was all over her like a rash. "Hello, boy." She bent down and picked him up. "I like having you here, but I think you should go back to your real mummy. What do you think?"

Elvis wriggled, so she put him down and made a fuss of him before feeding him.

After her shower, Charlotte went to her computer and researched Abigail's social-media profiles. Sure enough, there were lots of photos of Elvis on her Instagram account. So Charlotte packed up his bed and toys, and Grigore drove them to the nail bar. Charlotte picked up Elvis and gave him one last cuddle. "Maybe I should get my own doggy, Elvis. What do you think?"

Elvis wagged his tail.

Before getting out of the car, Charlotte looked through the window of the salon to see if Abigail was free. She was sat side-on at a table by the window. Abigail was painting the woman's nails, and Charlotte screwed her eyes up slightly because the woman having her nails done looked awfully familiar.

Charlotte did a double take, then moved away from the car window. It was Jessica. She couldn't miss her. She was so much taller and bulkier than most women. She dwarfed Abigail.

"Zomething wrong?" Grigore asked.

"The woman sitting in the window is one of the people of interest in the Hubbard murders."

"Suspicious, no?"

"Yes, very. I'll wait until she's gone. It could just be a coincidence, but I can't be sure."

Charlotte texted Angus. *Did Jessica have manicured nails when we saw her at the care home?*

A reply came by return. *Not that I remember. Why?*

I'll tell you later.

Elvis curled up on the seat opposite and went to sleep.

Eventually, Jessica left the salon. Charlotte left it

another five minutes before picking up Elvis and entering the salon.

The smell of acetone hit her the moment she went in. There were several people inside, but she recognised Abigail from her Instagram photos. "Abigail? I'm Charlotte Lockwood. I've been looking after Elvis since Andrew was killed."

Abigail was sitting behind the till, and stood up straight away. She saw Elvis, and stretched out her arms. "Oh my God, is that really my Elvis?"

Elvis went berserk, yapping and wriggling to get out of Charlotte's arms. Charlotte handed him over and he licked Abigail's face. "Oh, Elvie baby, I've missed you so much!"

Eventually, Elvis calmed down and Grigore brought in his bed and toys.

"Thank you so much for giving him back," Abigail gushed. "I hated giving him up. I don't know how I can ever thank you."

"Actually, there's something you could tell me. The customer with you just before I came in – do you know her?"

Abigail thought for a moment. "No, I've never seen her before. She was friendly, though. Nice lady: she said she works in a care home. I gave her ten percent off, like I do for all keyworkers. That's a job I could never do."

"She's not a regular here, then?"

Abigail shook her head. "No. I'm good at remembering customers. Unless she's been in on a Monday: that's my day off. Why?"

Charlotte smiled. "It doesn't matter. What did she talk about? She told you where she worked, anything else?"

"Yeah, she talked about her job a bit. She seemed sad, and she mentioned it was three years since her brother died of an overdose. She came in to try and cheer herself up."

"Did she say anything else about her brother?"

"I thought it best to change the subject, so we talked about the weather."

Charlotte looked down at Elvis, who was curled up on Abigail's chair. "It didn't take him long to pinch your seat."

"I don't mind; I'm so happy to have him back. Funny, you're the second person who's come in to ask me something lately. A man came a few days ago. Adam, or something. Nice chap."

"Angus."

Abigail's eyes widened. "That's right."

"He's my colleague."

"So you're looking into who killed Robert and his brother?"

Charlotte nodded.

"I hope you catch whoever did it. It was finished between Robert and me but I didn't want him dead."

"So do I." Charlotte left, rather sorry to say goodbye to Elvis. She'd liked having him around.

In the back of the Bentley, she phoned Angus. He picked up immediately.

"I've just given Elvis back to Abigail, and I saw Jessica Shaw in there, having her nails done."

There was a moment of silence. "Really?" said Angus. "She doesn't live or work anywhere near that place."

"I know, and I think that's odd too. What would Jessica be trying to do? Jessica told Abigail that her brother had died of a drug overdose three years ago."

"That definitely needs looking into."

"I'm going to try and hack her Wi-Fi again. I want to know what she's up to."

"I'll come and pick you up. If it's going to take some time, you'll need a car that blends into the background."

An hour later, they were parked near Jessica's house in Angus's VW Golf. Charlotte opened her laptop and started her advanced hacking program. This time it was new and improved, with extra dictionary words and common password formats.

"It's very suspicious that someone unconnected to the computing industry has such a strong password on their Wi-Fi. I mean, care workers do a vital and important job. But why would a care worker need a password like that?" She narrowed her eyes.

Angus looked at her. "I totally agree that it's suspicious. That, and her sudden appearance at a nail salon where the ex-girlfriend of a murdered man works. A man accused of catfishing. And she belongs to a Facebook group on the subject."

Five minutes later, the password still hadn't been cracked. If it took longer than twenty minutes, Charlotte wasn't sure what she would do.

She was looking at the screen when Angus spoke. "Other than through Facebook Messenger, how does Katrina know Jessica?"

"They don't know each other in real life," Charlotte replied absently, still gazing at the screen.

"Then why is Katrina knocking on Jessica's door?"

That made Charlotte look up. "What?"

Sure enough, Katrina was standing outside Jessica's front door. The door opened and Jessica let Katrina in.

"What the..." Charlotte reached to unbuckle her seatbelt.

Angus turned to her. "Where are you going?"

"I'm going in."

"Think about it, Charlotte. How are you going to explain that you know Katrina is there?"

"Well, Katrina knows you're investigating to get her off the hook, so she'd just think that you were investigating Jessica."

"We don't want Jessica knowing that, though, do we?" said Angus. "She'd probably think that you've been following her."

Charlotte sighed. "I see what you mean."

"Good. Carry on trying to get into her Wi-Fi. We can find out more about her that way."

"All right. But when I next see Katrina, I'm going to ask her if she's had any private contact with the people on Facebook. And she'd better not lie to me."

Ten minutes later, she still hadn't cracked the password. "They must be having some kind of meeting," she said, leaning back in her seat.

"It sure looks like it."

"We need to be a fly on the wall..." Charlotte said a few minutes later. "And now we can! My password cracker finally worked."

"Well done."

"She certainly had a complex password. A sixteen-character one, a mixture of uppercase, lowercase, symbols and numbers." Charlotte tapped away at the keyboard. "Now for my little program that sniffs around the network. Let's see what you're up to, Jessica."

Angus frowned. "What are you doing?"

"I'm checking whether she's got any smart gadgets with microphones I can hack. They're really easy to get into; no one ever changes the factory password."

Angus shook his head, looking incredulous. "You can hack someone's gadget and listen in on their microphone?"

"Oh yes. If they're connected to the home network and Wi-Fi, smart gadgets can be easily controlled. Not every gadget has a microphone. Some have video, though, so that would be really handy. We could see them as well as hear them." Charlotte's eyes glistened as she typed. "She's got a smart TV and a couple of smart speakers, but nothing with a microphone. That's disappointing. I can't locate her computer on the network either. That is strange."

An hour later, the front door opened and they saw Katrina come out, and right behind her was David: admin of the Facebook group and from the supermarket.

"I wasn't expecting that." Angus frowned. They must have been talking about the case. That's the only way they're connected."

Charlotte was too shocked to speak at first. "I can't believe she's been meeting them secretly. I'm going to visit Katrina and see if she'll tell me what they talked about."

Angus rolled his eyes. "I thought we agreed we weren't going to tell her that we were over here?"

"I won't, I promise. I'll just drop in and see if she mentions it. I'm now questioning everything she's ever told me."

"I don't think it's that surprising they are meeting. She doesn't have to tell you everything she does you know."

Charlotte's eyes narrowed. "What do you mean?"

"I mean, you might have paid for her lawyer, but she can go about her day without telling you everyone she meets."

"Not when she's meeting people relevant to the murder she's a suspect for." They stared at each other for a moment. "Hang on. What exactly do you mean when you said 'You might have paid for her lawyer'?"

Angus shrugged. "Just that paying for a lawyer is all very well, but it doesn't mean you own her."

"I know that." Charlotte shifted in her seat. There was a long pause. "We should still see what they were talking about. It could be relevant to the case."

Angus sighed. "All right. You'll only get Grigore to drive you if I don't."

Charlotte smiled and nodded. When they arrived, Katrina's car wasn't on the drive, and when Charlotte knocked on the door, there was no answer. She wasn't replying to her texts or answering calls either. She huffed and got back into Angus's car.

"Maybe she's out shopping or something," said Angus. "Haven't you got a tracking device on her?" He grinned. "Which reminds me – whatever you're using to track me, remove it." He took out his mobile phone, unlocked it, and handed it to her.

Charlotte stared at him and opened her mouth to speak.

"Don't even try to deny it," warned Angus.

Charlotte lifted her chin. "I would never lie to you, Angus." She took the phone. "It's just the 'Find my Friend' app. You can track me too. Don't you remember? We synched."

"No," he said, in a serious voice.

"Oh well, you just have to delete this app here."

He took his phone back, pressed the icon and deleted it, then put the phone in the side pocket of the door. "Home, then?"

"I suppose so. Look, why don't you stay for dinner? Helena's cooking, and she's been nagging me to invite you again. It's pork goulash; you'll love it. It tastes insanely good. And you haven't come to dinner for ages." Charlotte had a pleading look in her eyes, and Angus knew he would find it difficult to refuse her anything when she asked him like that.

Helena was delighted to see Angus. "You refuse too much. I think you no like my cooking," she said when they'd arrived.

Angus shifted from foot to foot and put his hands in his pockets. "I just don't want to take liberties. I don't expect to be fed every time I'm here."

Helena waved her hands. "Pah, ve no mind. You stay every day if you like."

"Absolutely," agreed Charlotte.

"You go sit at table, I bring food."

They did as she asked, and not long afterwards, Grigore came in and sat down. He took out his phone and buried his head in it.

Helena brought the food in and served everyone. Grigore was given an extra-large portion, and even put his phone away while he ate.

The pork goulash did taste really good, and it was served with creamy mashed potatoes and steamed cabbage.

"There," Helena said, when she finally sat down with her plate. She took a bite of food, then turned to Charlotte. "I vatch *Viper's Nest* last night. Your bastard ex-husband still arrogant bastard," she spat.

Charlotte looked down at her plate, then met Helena's eyes. "Did he part with any of his hard-earned cash?"

"No, he just act arrogant and put people down."

Charlotte grinned. "No change there, then!"

They heard a ping from the kitchen. "Sorry, iz my phone," said Helena. "I get lots of text from man I met."

Everyone looked at Helena, and Grigore's eyes narrowed. "Who zis man?" he demanded.

Helena picked up her glass of water. "Just man who

help get woman from refuge new home. Nothing like that ... yet." She smiled.

"Tell me where he live," Grigore demanded.

Charlotte interceded, "It's all right, Grigore. Helena has promised to tell me about any man she decides to date, so that I can do a full background check. No stone will go unturned."

Helena turned to Angus. "God help him."

Angus laughed. "Are you involved with a local refuge?"

Helena and Charlotte exchanged glances, and Charlotte gave a tiny nod. "I work at refuge a day a week," Helena replied. "It hidden on Dartmoor."

"Is that because you spent time in a refuge yourself?"

"Yez, I help set it up. Charlotte, she pay for it."

"Helena, you're not supposed to tell anyone that!" Charlotte scolded.

Helena shrugged. "Mr Angus, he no tell anyone. You trust him. Who he tell?"

"I haven't got anyone to tell." He turned to Charlotte. "You paid for a women's refuge?"

"She still pay," said Helena. "It cost lots money."

Angus put his fork down. "I can't think of a more worthy cause. I dealt with plenty of domestic violence in the police. It's endemic."

Charlotte stood up and picked up the empty water jug. "I don't like talking about what I spend my money on. It's up to me and no one else." She walked out of the room.

"She no stay mad long," said Helena. "She do many good zings vith her money, not like her bastard ex-husband who go on holiday all time and buy big car and yacht."

Charlotte popped her head around the door. "He's bought a yacht? Also, I have a big car. So you can't criticise him for that."

"Yez, but not biggest yacht in marina. He no rich enough."

"Good. Anyway, he always got seasick." Charlotte disappeared into the kitchen again, then reappeared with a refilled jug and sat down. "How long until your race, Angus?" she asked as she stabbed at a piece of goulash, clearly changing the subject.

"Next Sunday. I'm pretty much there with the training. Just one more long run, and I'll be ready."

"What time does the race start?"

"Ten am. Why, are you thinking of coming along?" Angus laughed, then straightened his face when she nodded.

"I thought I'd come along to cheer you on."

Angus sat back in his chair and smiled. "If you're not doing anything else, I'd appreciate it."

Chapter Twenty-One

The next morning, Charlotte came to Angus's house to work. "I'm really concerned about Katrina; I still haven't heard from her," she said, when she arrived. "She's never ghosted me for this long."

"Ghosted?" Angus asked, with a frown.

"Not replied to my messages."

"Ah. You could try seeing if she's at home again?"

"I've just sent Grigore to see if she's at work, and he'll call me with an update as soon as. There's something else too... Last night, I checked out Abigail's Instagram account; I wondered if she'd posted about Elvis. She hadn't, but look at this." Charlotte tapped on her phone, and held it out to Angus.

The phone showed a photo of Abigail and Robert Hubbard, sitting in a beer garden. They were behind a table, heads close together, smiling. It was a bright, sunny day. Both wore sunglasses and held up drinks: a pint of beer and a white wine. Underneath, she'd typed: Bank Holiday fun #BankHoliday #Drinkies #Pub #Exeter #Devon #RiverExe #TheSwan #Lovelife #sunshine #BeerGarden

"When was this posted?" asked Angus.

"A year ago, well before they broke up, but look at that hashtag: #*TheSwan*."

Angus looked at Charlotte's excited face. "The Swan pub, where Robert's body was found." He thought for a moment. "It might just be a coincidence. That pub is popular, and it was a while ago. Did they go there often?"

"From the photos, they went there a lot," Charlotte replied. "Did Abigail have an alibi for Robert's murder?"

Angus thought back to his meeting with Abigail. "I didn't ask, but I was the one who broke the news to her that Robert was dead. She was shocked. If she was pretending, and she did murder him, she's a very good actress. I'd be surprised if she did it."

Charlotte eyed him. "I'm going to ask you a question, and I don't want you to take it personally, okay?"

Angus raised his eyebrows. "Go on..."

"Are you just saying that because she's a young, attractive woman?"

"What?" Angus frowned. "You think I'd be influenced by something like that?"

"I don't know. Would you?"

Angus studied Charlotte in silence. "I don't often get offended, but I thought you'd know me better by now."

Charlotte sighed. "All right, well, let's go and talk to her."

Angus nodded. "I think that's a very good idea."

Half an hour later, they approached the nail salon. Abigail had seen them walking over, and was ready to receive them when they got entered. It was clearly a quiet time; there was no one else in there except Elvis, who was sitting on his bed behind the counter. As soon as he saw Angus, he growled, then started barking.

Abigail laughed. "He hardly ever gets upset with anyone. Have you come to check on him?"

Angus gave the dog a long stare. "No. We've come to talk to you about Robert."

Abigail picked Elvis up, put him in the staff area, and closed the door. The barking stopped. She sat on the high stool behind the counter. "Sure. What did you want to ask?"

Angus pushed up his glasses and took out his notebook. "Did you meet Robert on the night he was murdered?" He was bluffing to see if she admitted anything.

"Er, no." Abigail's smile vanished.

"Come on, we know you met him. We're not accusing you of killing him, but you did meet him. Didn't you?"

Abigail stared at Angus, then glanced at Charlotte, who gave her a look of encouragement. "All right, yes, I did meet him. He messaged me on WhatsApp."

"What did he say?" Angus asked.

"He said he needed to talk to me about Andrew being murdered."

"Where did you meet him?"

"At The Swan pub, in the beer garden. He didn't want to go inside."

"What time was this?"

"About ten thirty."

Angus made a note. "And was there anyone else sitting nearby?"

A brief laugh. "No, it was freezing that night. We didn't talk long because I was so cold."

"What did he want?"

"He was a mess. I've never seen him like that before. When we were together, he was always so self-assured. So steady, you know? But he was scared that night, really scared. He said Andrew had been killed because someone thought Andrew was him. He felt guilty about that, but he knew they'd be out to get him too."

"Did he know who was after him?"

"He said someone had been threatening him but they'd never identified themselves. He thought it might have been one of the drug gangs he was involved with, but he wasn't sure. He said they'd been sending him messages through a private messaging app."

"I know about those," said Charlotte. "They're phone apps like WhatsApp, programmed especially by and for gangs to use. They have their own encryption, so governments and police can't hack them or know what they're up to."

"So it's likely that whoever was after Robert was in a gang?" Angus asked.

"It looks like it."

He turned back to Abigail. "What else did you talk about?"

"Not much. He said the police had offered him protection, but they wanted him to give them the names of all the people he'd been working with, and he couldn't do that. He said they'd all kill him before this other person could. I told him he was reaping what he'd sown, and this had been a long time coming."

She sat silent, remembering.

Angus looked at his notebook. "What time did you leave?"

"I'm not sure. We only talked for about twenty minutes. I told him he needed to help himself and cooperate with the police, but he said he couldn't."

"Why was he meeting you, then?" Charlotte asked.

"He was warning me; he'd been contacting everyone close to him. He said he still cared about me." She looked up at them. "He was still alive when I left him in the beer garden, I swear. I had no reason to kill him. I own this place now, and I've moved on. I'm in a good place. Why would I jeopardise that?"

Charlotte and Angus looked at each other. "Was there no one else at all in the beer garden?" asked Angus. "Did anyone overhear you, or did you see anyone acting suspiciously?"

"Not that I saw. I mean, it was dark, but it was quiet at the pub, and we didn't get drinks or go inside. I don't even remember anyone walking past."

Angus put his notebook in his pocket. "Thanks for talking to us. If you think of anything, however small, call me." He handed her one of his cards.

Outside, they walked the short distance to Angus's car. "Do you believe her?" Charlotte asked.

"I'm not sure. I was convinced she was telling the truth before, but she didn't tell me about the meeting."

"Technically, she was. She just didn't mention that she'd met him."

Angus put his hands in his pockets. "She met Robert on the night he was killed, near where he was found, and she swears she didn't kill him. He was killed with a hammer blow to the head. It's certainly a method that a woman of her size could have used. We have to tell Woody. If there is any forensic evidence that could point to her, he'll have it."

Charlotte frowned. "But she didn't have a motive."

"Not that we know of. She could be hiding one." Angus took out his phone and called Woody. It went to voicemail, so he left a message.

They got into the car. "Are we going home?" asked Charlotte.

"Not yet. I want to see if Abigail does a runner."

"That's a good idea. If she did murder Robert, then now that she's admitted meeting him that night, she'll bolt. How long do you think we should wait?"

"Half an hour, I reckon."

Forty-five minutes later, Abigail hadn't bolted. They'd seen a few people go into the salon, including another member of staff, and they could see her working. "I think we should go," said Angus, starting the engine. "If she was going to do a runner, she'd have done it by now."

Charlotte's phone rang. "Katrina, finally!" She accepted the call, and held the phone to her ear. "Hello, darling, I've been trying to get hold of you. How are you?"

There was silence, then a muffled noise.

"Hello? Katrina?"

"Help me, Charlotte, she's got me..."

"Katrina, are you all right? Katrina?"

The call ended.

"What's wrong?" Angus asked.

"She said, 'Help me, she's got me.' I think she's in trouble." Charlotte's face went pale. She dialled Katrina's number, but it went straight to voicemail. She began typing a text.

"Be careful," said Angus. "If she is in trouble and someone has got her, your text might alert them. Just tell her to call you."

Charlotte nodded, deleted her first words, and typed:
Call me ASAP. C x

"Did you hear anything in the background that might help us locate her?"

"No, just some muffled noise, like she was moving around."

"Do you have tracking software on her phone?"

Charlotte shook her head.

"And she said 'She's got me'? Are you sure about that? She didn't say *he*?"

"No, it was definitely *she*."

"So from the suspects we know about, it can't be Abigail because she's in the salon in front of us. The only other woman is –"

"Jessica," they both said at the same time.

Charlotte's eyes narrowed. "I knew she was hiding something."

Angus shook his head. "We don't know it's her."

"I'd put a large quantity of money on it," Charlotte said decisively.

"We'll go to Jessica's house; it's not far away. Can you ask Grigore to drive to Katrina's house and see if she's there? Tell him that if he needs to jimmy the door to get in, I said he can do it." Charlotte nodded and picked up her phone.

Angus parked near Jessica's house and they got out. When Angus knocked on the door, there was no answer. He knocked louder, and looked through the letterbox, but there was no one around.

"Maybe she's at work?" Charlotte suggested.

"Call the care home and ask to speak to her."

Charlotte found the number and dialled. It was picked up after a few rings. "Hi, could I speak to Jessica, please?"

"I'm sorry, it's her day off," said a pleasant female voice. "Can anyone else help? What was it about?"

"Do you know what she had planned today? I'm her friend, and I wanted to meet up with her, but she's not answering her phone. Can I check it with you?" Charlotte's heart was racing. She forced herself not to think about the danger Katrina could be in.

"Let me just get her number, love. I don't have it with me." The line went quiet and Charlotte could hear general shuffling noises. A short time later, the phone was picked up. "This is the number I have..." Charlotte mimed writing to Angus and scribbled the number down in his notebook as the woman read it out. "Is that the number you've got, love?"

"Yes, it is, thanks," said Charlotte. "I'll try her again."

"All right, my love, bye now."

Charlotte ended the call. "She's not at work, and they don't know what she's doing today."

Angus had moved to the front window. "I don't like the sound of that. Too many things are pointing to her."

Charlotte walked towards the side of the house. "We need to get in and see what she's been up to. They might be in here..."

Angus moved past her and tried the large wooden gate that led to the back garden. It opened, and they went through.

The back garden was small, with artificial grass, a small shed at the back and trees and bushes that made it secluded.

They went to the shed straight away, but it was locked. There was no window, so Angus pulled hard at the door but it wouldn't budge. Charlotte knocked. "Katrina? Katrina, are you there?" she said softly.

There was a thump from inside, and Angus and Charlotte looked at each other.

"I've got something that should open this, in the boot. Wait here." Angus disappeared, and came back a minute later with a crowbar.

Charlotte stared at him. "You carry a crowbar in your boot?"

"You never know when one might come in handy," Angus replied. He inserted the crowbar in the small gap between door and frame, and heaved. After a couple of goes, the door swung open.

On the floor was Katrina, her hands and feet tied together. Her eyes were half-closed and her head lolled, but she appeared uninjured.

"Oh my goodness, Katrina!" Charlotte cried. She ran over to her, crouched down beside her and supported her head. "Katrina, where is Jessica? Where is she?"

Angus untied her hands and ankles, then made two brief calls: one for an ambulance, and one to Woody.

He put the phone in his pocket. "Stay with her, Charlotte. I'm going to see if Jessica is at home."

Charlotte sat on the floor with Katrina, cradled her head and waited for the ambulance to come.

Chapter Twenty-Two

Angus approached Jessica's house, and took a crowbar with him. The uPVC back door was locked, so he smashed its window. Jessica had left the key in the lock inside, so he put his hand through, turned it and entered.

Inside, the kitchen was spotlessly clean. He went through to the hallway and checked the other downstairs rooms. The lounge was first, dominated by a brown corner sofa with too many scatter cushions. A small TV sat in the corner and the room was decorated with dark-purple-feature wallpaper. The dining room faced the street, and held a round table with four chairs.

Next, he went upstairs. The first room was the bathroom, then the master bedroom. Jessica's bed was a double, covered with a plain white duvet, and there was a bedside table and a wardrobe.

Finally, the spare bedroom. Angus paused for a moment, taking it in. It was an office rather than a bedroom, with a desk, an office chair and a computer. But Angus was interested in the main wall. A conspiracy board covered it.

Unlike Charlotte's boards, which were uncomplicated but effective, this was huge, with large and small pieces of paper stuck to it. Some were photos of people, some small maps, some written statements. Lots of string joined different sections.

Angus scanned it, trying to figure out what it was all about. There were three pictures in the centre: Robert Hubbard, Andrew Hubbard, and Abigail. But a big cross had been drawn over Robert and Andrew's pictures.

Angus's eyebrows shot up, then he took out his phone and called Charlotte. "Jessica isn't here. But she's Andrew and Robert's killer, and I think she's after Abigail next."

"What? How do you know that? I'll call Abigail and warn her. Should you go and see if she's okay?"

"Jessica might come back here. Is Katrina awake? Has she said anything?"

"No, she's drifting in and out of consciousness. I'm sure she's been drugged."

Angus heard a siren in the background. "Can you hear that?" Charlotte said. "Hopefully, that's the ambulance. If it is, we can go straight to Abigail."

"I'll be down in a moment." Angus took photos of the wall, then went down as the siren peaked outside, then ceased. He led the ambulance crew through to the shed, and then his phone rang.

"Mate, we've got a few logistical problems," said Woody. "We'll be a few minutes. Do what you can, yeah?"

He went into the garden just as Katrina was being stretchered out. Charlotte was just behind her. "I only hope it's something like Rohypnol and not poison," she said. "I want to go with her, but they won't let me."

153

"Did you get through to Abigail?" he asked.

"No, she didn't pick up at the salon. I don't have her mobile number."

"We need to find her. Jessica's after her."

Charlotte's brow furrowed. "But why?"

"I'm not sure, but Jessica's been planning this for a while. There's a conspiracy wall in her spare room, and she's definitely after her. We need to warn her."

"Does she have a computer in there?" Charlotte jerked a thumb at the house.

"Yes, there's a desktop in the spare room."

"I'll go in and see what I can find while you go to the salon."

When Angus got to the nail salon, it was still open. He burst through the door, making the single customer waiting stare at him. "Is Abigail here?" he asked.

The woman's eyes grew even wider. "I've been waiting for ages. Abigail was here, then she said she'd just make herself a coffee. But that was twenty minutes ago. I'm not sure what she's doing."

Angus headed straight for the door that led to the staff area. It was deserted, and the back door to the shop was open. Outside, no one was around.

Angus put his hand to his forehead. He took out his phone and rang Charlotte. "She's not here. I think Jessica's got her."

Charlotte went into Jessica's spare room and switched on the computer. As soon as it had started up, she was met with a prompt to enter a password. She tried a few commonly used ones, but they didn't let her in. If Jessica had a complex

WiFi password, she'd probably have a complex computer password too.

Then she looked at Jessica's conspiracy wall again, looking for clues... She tried her brother's name *Christopher* and it let her in straight away.

She opened the email program. There weren't many; mostly junk, or from her employer.

Charlotte searched the installed apps to see if there was anything interesting, and noticed Find My Device. "I wonder if I can find where you are, Jessica. I bet you have your mobile phone with you. Let's see..."

The app opened and asked for a password. "Password... I bet you have it stored in your browser. Yes, you do." The app opened fully and Charlotte clicked on the option to find Jessica's mobile phone. "Thank you, password keychains."

The program froze for a moment, then about thirty seconds later, displayed the location.

Charlotte dialled Angus, who picked up straight away. "I've got into her computer and I'm able to trace her phone. Get to The Swan pub; she's there. I'll let Mark know too. Where is he?"

"Delayed. But yes, phone him and tell him too."

Angus tried not to break the speed limit getting to The Swan. He did his best, and he winced every time the speedometer needle went over the legal limit. When he was a few miles away, Charlotte called again. He pressed a button to answer hands-free.

"She's on the move," said Charlotte. "She's heading towards a farm. Take the next lane after the pub, towards Faraway Farm."

Angus followed Charlotte's instructions and saw Jessica's car ahead, parked in a lay-by.

"I can see her car, she's parked up." He pulled up behind the car, blocking her in.

"Be careful..." Charlotte said before he ended the call.

The place where Jessica had chosen to park was blanketed by trees, making it darker than the rest of the lane. He looked around; Jessica wasn't in the car, or close by. The back seat of the car was empty too. Then he tried the boot, it was unlocked.

It took a moment for him to register what he saw. Abigail. She was inside, unconscious but breathing.

"Step away from my car." Jessica was standing a short distance away, with a spade in her hand. Her eyes seemed glazed and her face wore a stoney expression. Angus hoped she gave up easily because she was tall and large and he wasn't sure he fancied his chances against her.

"It's over, Jessica. The police are on their way; they'll be here any moment. We've found Katrina."

"This is not over. Not until she's dead." Jessica jerked her head towards the boot.

Angus moved to the side of the car. "Stay there!" Jessica shouted.

"Or what?" Angus took a step forward. "You can run for it, but where will you hide? I'll catch you before you get to that gate." He moved another step closer.

"She helped to kill my brother. I have to kill her."

"Your brother? How? Tell me what happened."

"Robert sold him drugs. He died of an overdose." She stared at him breathing heavily. "Robert killed him." She gave a sob when she stopped speaking.

Angus decided not to move forward again; keeping her

talking would be the best thing to do. "When did this happen?"

"A few years ago."

"Is that why you killed Robert?"

"Yes!" she spat. "He deserved it!"

Angus considered what to say next. "Did you mean to kill Andrew?" he asked, at last.

She sighed. "That was a mistake. But then again, it meant Robert knew what it was like to have a brother killed for no reason."

"But why Abigail? She's never done anything to hurt you."

"She knew he was selling drugs. She could have stopped him."

Angus took a deep breath. "Abigail wasn't responsible for Robert or what Robert did, any more than Andrew."

"She knew about it. She could have done something."

In the distance, a police siren wailed. Jessica tensed, and Angus thought she was going to run. But she dropped the spade, sank onto the ground, and put her head in her hands.

Woody and a couple of other officers arrived and arrested Jessica, then put her into a patrol car.

Woody took Angus a few feet away from the car. "Well done," he said. "Was it Charlie who found her?"

Angus smiled. "Good guess. I have no idea how, but I'm sure she'll tell us soon enough. Something to do with Jessica's computer."

Woody shook his head and grinned. "Yep, it's always the computer with her."

The ambulance arrived a few minutes later, and after checking her over, took Abigail away.

Chapter Twenty-Three

Charlotte entered The Ivy restaurant in Exeter and saw Katrina sitting at the far end of the room, looking dreamily out of the window.

She walked over to her. "Hello, darling, how are you?"

A smile spread across Katrina's lips. "Hello, you. It's wonderful to see you again so soon." She stood up and kissed Charlotte on the cheeks, and they sat down together.

Katrina put her hands on the table. "I can't thank you enough for everything you've done. And Angus too. I'm so glad it's all over."

Charlotte smiled. "I'm just glad you're okay. I don't know what I'd have done if Jessica had killed you." She puffed out a breath and shook her head. "If you hadn't called me, she'd have got to Abigail. How did you call me? Your hands were tied."

"She drugged me first. I had a few minutes before they kicked in properly and when she first locked me in the shed. She must have tied me up when I passed out. She was probably going to kill me, too, just like Robert and Andrew." Katrina shuddered.

The waiter came over and took their order. "Tell me what happened," said Charlotte, once he had gone.

Katrina took a deep breath. "Jessica called me a few times, then asked me over. She said it was a meeting to help support people who'd been catfished; she'd invited David the group admin too. We talked about Robert and the case too."

She sighed. "But the second time I went to her house, it was just me. She kept asking about you and Angus. Not just general stuff, but details about what you'd found out in your investigation. That made me suspicious, and I told her I didn't know much. I used her toilet, partly to get some thinking time because I felt uneasy. The door to the spare room was open, and I sneaked in and saw – I saw that wall. I don't know if she saw me, or heard me, or if I'd given myself away downstairs."

"That must have been when she slipped something in your drink," said Charlotte.

"Yes."

Charlotte leaned forward and touched Katrina's hand. "You were so brave, and thank goodness you got to your phone. She's going to rot in prison now, and you're free. And I'll always be here for you."

Katrina nodded. "I know," she said, with a smile. "How did she kill Robert and Andrew? She'd been working in the care home when Andrew was killed in Sidmouth..."

"My brother Mark said she had been on night shift but admitted slipping sleeping pills into all the residents' evening cocoa. She'd checked they were all asleep and snuck out at one am and driven to Sidmouth. Apparently she'd parked her car away from the care home and out of sight of CCTV but deleted the recordings for that night anyway. She'd been very calculating about it all. She said she saw you leave after Andrew had thrown you out. Then knocked on his door, went inside and killed him."

"And had it been a mistake to kill Andrew instead of Robert?"

Charlotte nodded.

Katrina sat motionless as she took it all in. "What about Robert's murder?"

"She'd been following Abigail, looking for an opportunity to kill her, and followed her to The Swan pub the night she met Robert and the night he'd been killed. When Abigail left, she'd knocked him on the head with a hammer as he walked over the bridge."

"That's just horrible. How can anyone do that?"

"She was very close to her brother; she felt she was getting justice for him."

They sat silent for some time before Charlotte took a white envelope from her bag and put it on the table. "This is for you."

Katrina shook her head and pushed the envelope towards Charlotte. "I can't take more money from you; you've already given me back what I lost."

"It's not money: it's a holiday. I thought you could do with a complete break. Two weeks at an exclusive resort in Jamaica, for you and a friend."

Katrina's eyes opened very wide and her hand went to her mouth. "Oh my goodness, I've always wanted to go there. Thank you!" She took the envelope and put it in her handbag.

Charlotte smiled. "I remembered; that's why I chose it."

"When I come back from Jamaica, we must make meeting here a regular thing."

"I'd love that." Charlotte looked out of the window onto the street.

Katrina tapped her arm. "Penny for them?"

Charlotte turned back to her. "Sorry, I was just thinking about Angus. He's out training now for that race, and it's starting to rain."

Katrina rolled her eyes. "So that's why he's not here. I was hoping you'd bring him along."

Charlotte hid a smile. She hadn't invited Angus, and she'd arranged the meeting when she knew he was busy. She didn't feel guilty, though. She'd promised Angus that she would never try and match him up with one of her friends. Or that was what she'd told herself when she was justifying her action. And she wasn't going to encourage Katrina either. If they wanted to contact each other directly, that was up to them, but she'd have no part in it. "Angus said to tell you he's glad everything is sorted now."

"That's kind. He's so much nicer than Idris. I can't understand how you stayed with him for so long. He's such an idiot in that TV show too. Have you watched?"

Charlotte remembered the newspaper she'd bought earlier, and pulled it out of her bag. "No, I haven't, but I found this newspaper columnist's comments hilarious."

She turned a few pages and read it out.

"New Viper has no teeth. Viewers around the UK were eager to watch the new series of *Viper's Nest* last week and meet the new Viper: Idris Beavin, tech multimillionaire. However, many found him crass and deliberately rude to the entrepreneurs vying for his support, and he failed to offer money to any of the contestants. One wonders how they found such a man, and whether he can be parted with any of his cash. Time will tell..."

Katrina started to quietly giggle and Charlotte had a broad smile.

When the waiter brought their coffees. Katrina held up her coffee cup. "To friends."

"To friends," said Charlotte, clinking cups with her.

On Sunday, Charlotte, Helena and Grigore stood near the finish line of the Grizzly race. It was on the esplanade in Seaton, a small seaside town twenty miles east of Exeter. The race had started four hours earlier, and they'd cheered as Angus ran past the first-mile post.

Charlotte had painted several banners. The first had "Go Angus!" written on it, and they'd held it up and cheered as he ran past.

Grigore had then driven them to different parts of the route over the next few hours. They waited for Angus and cheered him along each time, then moved to the next point. The finish was their fifth and final stop.

Each banner had something different written on it. At the seven-mile point, the banner read "Finishing is your only option."

At the eleven-mile point, it read "Run like you stole something."

At the fifteen-mile point, it read "You run better than the government."

All of them had made Angus laugh, and he'd waved at them with a grin. Charlotte had considered putting "I'm checking out your backside as you run past." But had decided against it. She didn't want to freak him out.

Now, at the finish, the last banner read "Your PE teacher, Mr Richards, would be proud." It had taken Charlotte nearly an hour on the internet to find the name of Angus's school PE teacher, finally tracking it down on a school reunion Facebook page.

A steady stream of runners poured down the steep Castle Hill to the finish line, and crowds of people were cheering everyone on. Charlotte looked at her phone. Her app indicated that Angus was about half a mile away.

Helena glanced at the phone. "Does he know you track him?"

"No. Well, I deleted an app that tracked him. This is a different one. Just for today."

Helena snorted. "Is creepy you track him."

Charlotte smiled at Helena. "Maybe one day it will come in handy. You never know."

In the distance, Angus appeared, running towards the finish line, and they began jumping up and down and cheering. He saw their banner as he approached and smiled. He looked tired, and he was covered in mud from head to toe. So different to his normal clean and smart appearance.

"Come on, let's see him on the other side of the finish line," said Charlotte as he passed.

They moved past the finish line, and watched as Angus was given a medal, a foil wrap, and a drink and snack.

Farther on, the local fire brigade were there with a small engine, ready to hose off the runners. Charlotte grinned. Angus was always clean, neat and tidy, and sure enough he joined the queue to get hosed down.

When he came out the other side, dripping wet, Charlotte hugged him briefly and kissed him on the cheek. "Well done, you were brilliant! I can't believe you ran all that way."

"Neither can I." He smiled, and didn't let go when she started to pull away. "That wasn't much of a hug, come here!" He hugged her tighter.

"You've made me all wet!" she said, laughing.

Angus let go and looked down. "You're right, but at least it isn't mud."

They were interrupted by someone approaching them. It was Graham, on crutches, with his left leg in a plaster cast.

Graham stopped, leant on his right crutch, and offered his hand to Angus. "Well done, mate, you were brilliant. And your time is nothing to be ashamed of."

Angus took his hand briefly and Charlotte took a discreet step backwards to allow the men to talk.

"Thanks, it would have been better if you'd been there, but maybe next year?"

Graham nodded. "I fully intend to be exactly where you are this time next year. When I'm ready to start training again, I'll give you a bell."

"You make sure you do. It's much better training with you than alone."

"Well, the cast comes off in a month, and they've already assigned me a physio, so I'm eager to get back to it when I can."

A few minutes later, Charlotte watched Graham hobble off and Angus came over to her. She'd been stood a few feet away.

"You should have stayed. I would have introduced you both." Angus looked over at Graham who he saw was with his wife.

"Don't worry, you can next time." Charlotte gestured towards Grigore and Helena, who were watching them from a short distance away.

"How did you find out my PE teacher's name?" Angus narrowed his eyes but he was smiling.

Charlotte pointed to herself with both hands. "Computer expert. How do you think? Anyway, I thought you might want a ride home after all that running?"

He paused, unsure. He wasn't used to accepting anything from her. Then the pain in his feet and legs reminded him this was no time to be defensive. "That's very thoughtful of you, and I'd love a ride home; my legs feel like jelly. In fact, would you mind chauffeuring me in my car, and keeping me company for a few hours? I'm tired, but the buzz of doing this will make it impossible to sleep."

Charlotte nodded. "All right. We can watch a film, and I'll order in pizza." She'd have to play it cool, but she was quite excited at the prospect of having Angus to herself.

"Perfect," he replied.

The End

* * *

DEAR READER, I hope you enjoyed the second in the series. It would be brilliant if you could leave a review because it helps readers find my books.

IF YOU WANT MORE from Charlotte and Angus, the third book is available to buy here.

Trouble with the Exe:

Charlotte's ex-husband, Idris, has been kidnapped, and his latest wife, Michelle, who also happens to be Charlotte's former best friend begs her to help find him before the kidnappers kill him.

Suzy Bussell

With a long list of people who Idris has upset, Charlotte and Angus must work together to try and figure out which of them took him, whilst not alerting the police.

When they start to pinpoint who might have done it, a twist of fate means Charlotte is put in mortal danger too.

SIGN up to my newsletter on my website to get a FREE Lockwood and Darrow short story.
http://www.suzybussell.com

Suzy xx

Acknowledgments

Many thanks as ever to my amazing and supportive husband and to Liz Hedgecock, my editor and mentor, who also writes mysteries - check her books out!

About the Author

Suzy started writing at the age of thirty when she penned her first story—a fan fiction—and then graduated on to writing her own characters and tales.

In 2019, she found herself unable to silence the persistent voices of Charlotte and Angus in her thoughts, their vivid characters forcing her hand to starting the 'Lockwood and Darrow' series.

Originally from Hertfordshire, she's called Devon home for two decades. Its picturesque landscapes and unique characters have embedded themselves in almost every story she's penned.

She has a background in computing and a keen interest in technology which naturally weaves its way into her plots to add a touch of modern intrigue. The world of technology has always fascinated her, and merging this with her passion for storytelling felt like a natural progression.

Currently, she lives close to the sea with an amazing and supportive husband, three sons, and two snowshoe cats. When she's not writing, she loves swimming and playing her violin.

Printed in Great Britain
by Amazon